These stories grab us by the thr[oat] ... Beautiful writing, complex chara[cters] ... but what strikes me the most is ... tell a story, as in the work of Alice Munro, in which the writer disappears and the story reads as if a free agent of its own making. With *Down to the Root*, David Dickson establishes himself as an essential North Carolina writer. More than any other contemporary writer I've read, David Dickson's stories evoke the grit and heart of Larry Brown.

—Ron Rash, author of *Serena*

David Dickson's relentless curiosity fuels his gritty storytelling, and this gut punch of a collection offers an unflinching stare into our shared humanity. Like the character Gus in Black Leather Jacket, Dickson values truth. *Root* is a brutally truthful, achingly beautiful book of short stories, with zero interest in romanticizing the hardscrabble South that this author knows intimately.

—Michel Stone, author of *The Iguana Tree* and *Border Child*

David Dickson solves the age old question of nature vs. nurture by proving that it's neither. He is a cross between Breece D'J Pancake and Charles Portis with a sliver of the old testament prophet Amos thrown in for the aftertaste.

—Tim Peeler, author of *West of Mercy*

The landscape of *Down to the Root* is familiar and haunting because David Dickson is impeccably honest and unafraid. Writers get to live twice, first in their bodies and then in their pages. Dickson possesses the best visceral qualities of a writer who does not flinch from the stark realities of our forlorn march through life's constant series of uncertainties. His powers of observation, manifested in the detailed particulars of his character's day to day existence, make these pages fulsome and vivid. His ear for dialect is just as keen, and I blasted through these stories, buoyed by surprise, delighted to know that a new talent has found his footing.

—Keith Flynn, author of *The Skin of Meaning*

David Dickson's stories are taut and compelling. There's real urgency in his voice, and he's got a great eye and a great ear. This is work I truly admire. It's from the heart.

—Steve Yarbrough, author of *Stay Gone Days*

Down to the Root

Stories

David C. Dickson

REDHAWK
PUBLICATIONS

ISBN: 978-1-959346-42-5 (Paperback)

Library of Congress Control Number: 2024933829

Any references to historical events, real people, or real places are used fictitiously. Names, characters, and places are products of the author's imagination.

Cover Concept: Jack Wells Dickson
Original Cover Layout: Jared Scott
Cover Design Execution: Melanie Zimmermann

Interior design by Robert T Canipe.

Printed in the United States of America.

First printing edition 2024.

Redhawk Publications
The Catawba Valley Community College Press
2550 Hwy 70 SE
Hickory NC 28602

Contents

Down to the Root

"Riding the Line," Raleigh *News and Observer Sunday Reader*.

"Lucky Break," Raleigh *News and Observer Sunday Reader*.

"The Jumping off Place," *North Carolina Literary Review*.

This book is dedicated to Frances Carolyn Wells who gave me life---three times.

"She ain't nothing but a whore, Kylmer."

His father spoke from the window of the truck, which was pulled off onto the shoulder of the road.

"I know how you feel about her. I can remember what it was like," he said and took a half-empty pack of cigarettes from his shirt pocket. "Getting your first steady piece of ass is a big deal. I just don't want to see you make a mistake, that's all."

"You mean like you did." The younger man's cheeks were flushed with anger and embarrassment, and he tried to look hard at his father.

"No, son. I never thought that. I only meant that you ain't but twenty-five years old, and she's the type of girl that could mess you up. I know more'n you think I do, I keep up with things when you ain't around. I talk with Grady and I know what's going on around here. I wouldn't be a very good father if I didn't tell you what I think about the situation."

Kylmer Hayes stepped away from the truck and shoved his hands deep into the pockets of his muddy jeans.

"Well, Pop, thanks for taking the time to stop by and be a good father."

He turned his back on his father's truck and began walking across the red clay yard. He could feel his father's gaze on his back as he covered the short distance to the porch of the small frame rental house.

"Nothing but a whore," he heard his father say, as he paused to scrape the mud off his boots.

"She fucks niggers, Kyle."

Kylmer didn't acknowledge the statement. Long seconds passed before the old man disengaged the clutch and steered the truck onto the county-maintained road. As his father drove away, Kylmer removed his boots, then looked in the direction of the oncoming traffic. The car's tires hissed on the wet pavement; the muffler belched loud flatulence of exhaust. He watched the spray rise from the road as the car passed, and hoped that the water would soak in. What little grass covered the yard was scorched yellow. The azalea bushes he'd planted next to the house were skeletal clumps of branches, and the garden was overgrown with dried weeds. The few things he'd done to fix the place up, trying to make it a place for Mary to call home, were dying.

She hadn't been around in more than a week, and Kylmer was beginning to wonder if she would come back at all this time. The few things she had left behind, clothes mostly, would be easy for her to replace. He missed her and spent most of his time at the house thinking of her, trying to remember how she smelled. A couple of times he took one of her dresses from the closet and held it to his face, inhaling her transient scent. He knew better than to go looking for her. If he found her, he might lose her forever. She knew that he would take her back, her and a baby.

"You may be right, Pop," he said to himself.

The phone rang inside the house, and he pulled off his wet socks before going inside to answer it. By the time he made it into the bedroom, the answering machine had picked up.

"Hi, Kylmer, give me a call whenever you get this message. Later."

He recognized Grady's voice. It had been a while since they had talked, but rather than call back immediately, he waited a few minutes. He stripped out of his filthy jeans and wet work shirt, and left them in a soured pile, then returned to the front room and looked out the screen door to the highway. No cars were in sight, so he stepped out on the porch wearing only his briefs. The knapsack was sitting where he'd left it, holding his day's find. He picked it up, and with one of the socks wiped at the mud caked on the bottom of it and took it into the house.

The rain had started back up and made a pleasant sound as it drummed the tin roof. He thought of the first morning the two of them shared in his bed. Early spring with the windows opened, they listened to the rain and drank orange juice and vodka. She got up to go to the kitchen and fix them another drink, and he lay in bed and watched her walk through the house. Standing on her toes stretching for the glasses in the cupboard, she innocently gave him a wonderful view of her backside, and of her legs, which looked long in proportion to her torso. As she turned to go to the refrigerator he admired her breasts, full and turned up on the end; he could imagine nothing more beautiful. It was about to become October and that April morning now seemed long ago.

He unzipped the sack and took out the artifacts wrapped in cloth. He had found some good things: two large axe heads about the size of his open palm, and a ceremonial pipe bowl. The axes were in perfect condition. Unlike most of the ones he tended to find, they were not rubbed smooth by river floods or chipped by plow points. The edges were sharp and the craftsmen's handiwork easily discernible. The blue-gray flint was rarely found in the area, and had an unusual flaked shape. Kylmer marveled at the precision with which ancient hands had made utilitarian objects into things of beauty. He had dug more than six feet down before uncovering them, through two layers of silt and loam, before coming to the dark layer of clay that encased the relics. The site was back in the woods, away from the tobacco fields and well off from the riverbank. Most diggers only worked around the periphery of plowed fields where the soil was easy to turn, so he felt secure in leaving exposed a larger area than normal.

There were laws that forbid what Kylmer loved to do. But he wasn't the only one trespassing. There were other artifact hunters who cared even less about laws than he. One family he knew of, a father and his three sons, carried shotguns to their digs and used them to intimidate others from leaving sites that held promise. The state archaeologists and college professors were just about as bad. They filled basement rooms at universities and warehouses with treasures some would die for, and if they had the chance, they would doggedly prosecute anyone found digging. Kylmer hated them for hoarding their finds, and for proceeding to excavate the sites that others had found.

"Goddamned Kylmer Hayes, if you're going to do something you might go to jail for, you ought to at least be doing something that'll get you rich," Mary once said when he returned from a trip to the mountains cut short by a confrontation with a land owner. She never seemed to be interested in the nature of his work. The admiration he had for the things he found had always been intensely personal, and he was reluctant to share it with anyone. But he had come to hope that she would someday accompany him on his digs and learn to value his vocation. As he unpacked the relics from his backpack, he wished for a moment that she were there and able to comprehend his gratification.

The pipe bowl was a special find. Carved from a soft dark gray stone, it had qualities unlike anything that he had seen before. The front of the bowl was adorned with a carving of a woman's face. The lips were parted and a small hole drilled through to the chamber. The interior of the bowl was free of soil, but was charred black by ancient fire. He knew a man who would pay a couple of hundred dollars for the objects, but he wasn't sure if he would sell the pipe. It wasn't a typical pipe for the area; it looked like something the moundbuilders might have made, and he wondered how it had gotten to Wilkes County. It was rare, and if he'd really needed the money, he might have taken it to a show. One was coming up in November, but he already had a big payday coming his way.

He planned to sell two Anasazi pots he'd found a couple of months earlier in New Mexico. They would bring more than he could earn in several years working in the furniture factory, or any other honest job around there. He believed the money would buy him time. Time to convince Mary that life with him could be comfortable and good, and to figure out what it was that she needed. If it were babies, the money would provide security. They could settle in, plant a garden, and raise a family. He had convinced himself that it could be.

He'd only found one other pipe in his years of digging, a small one made of clay, the type used by early settlers as trading items. He cherished it, and made a stem from a hollowed-out wooden dowel, using it occasionally to smoke pot. It had gotten misplaced, and oftentimes he awoke in the night wondering about the lost pipe. He figured that was how most of the items he found had originally come to rest. Careless mistakes made by people long dead, giving evidence of lives once lived. He always felt the same rush of exhilaration each time one of the ancient things was uncovered. It was as if some great mystery was about to be explained to him.

He left the objects on the table next to the front door and returned to the bedroom. He lay back on the bed and dialed Grady's number.

"Hey, Grady."

"Where you been, boy?"

"I've been out digging."

"Where abouts?"

"Over on the River at Tharpe's bottom. What's up?"

It sounded to Kylmer like someone was in the room with Grady as he spoke.

"I've got something I need you to help me with. Can you come over here about nine o'clock tonight?"

"I suppose I could. Is there anything you want me to bring?" He didn't know what else to say.

"No, not tonight. We'll talk about it when you get over here. All right?"

Kylmer had been reluctant to call and ask, but since they were on the phone, he couldn't stop himself. "Hey, Grady…have you heard anything from Mary?"

"Man, you need to quit messing around with her. She is a piece of shit, Kylmer, you'll see. Take my advice, brother man, and move on to something else."

"Why've you got to talk about her like that? She's your own sister, for Christ's sake"

"That's right, Kyle, and I know her better'n you do. She's a fuck-up, all right?"

He looked at the clock on the bedside table. It had started to get dark earlier, the summer days giving way to cool evenings. On top of the mountain, the trees were already showing signs of color. The sumac and Virginia creeper had turned blaze red in the valleys, and the last of the honeysuckle clung brown to the vines. It was a good time of year for digging. Most of the ground cover was starting to die off, and the late afternoon was cooler for his type of work.

Kylmer was excited about the site he was excavating. The hole was getting wider and, as he dug deeper, he kept finding quality artifacts. He'd dug in many places that yielded little other than a few bird points and broken pieces of pottery, but this place was different. There were no layers of midden, no mussel shells or other evidence of ancient refuse, and it had never been tilled. He wasn't sure about the location and what it had been used for, but he had already staked out two other sites in the area that yielded evidence of artifacts on the surface. He was encouraged about it and looked forward to each day's dig.

He went to the kitchen and took from the refrigerator a leftover piece of chicken. He poured a glass of tap water, then sat at the kitchen table and ate his meal. Food had never been much of a priority when she was around. He took most of his meals in the middle of the day, away from the house. She never seemed to have much of an appetite, especially after she started smoking cocaine. Right before she took off this last time, he noticed the gap between her legs was becoming more pronounced, and her breasts and behind were not as ample. Her eyes seemed too big, even when covered in sleep, like they had outgrown the sockets, or her face had shrunk around them.

He only smoked with her a couple of times, and never did like it. It went straight to the core of the brain and made him feel vulnerable, like he could lose himself to it. It frightened him to watch her take such pleasure from sucking on a pipe. It was evil shit, he told her. In the vapors that escaped her lips he thought he could see little pieces of her soul disappearing.

After finishing the cold food, he made his way to the bathroom. Running himself a hot tub, he decided to shave and take a long soak before going to Grady's. Her toothbrush was where she had left it on the sink. He thought about her perfect teeth, flawless except for the small gap between the two front ones. There was just enough space for him to put the tip of his tongue in between. He could almost smell her breath, the sweetness of which he could not compare to anything else. He wished she would come back, or stay gone forever.

The phone rang again just as he eased into the hot water. He sat back and surrendered to the heat, leaving the answering machine to take the message. He wondered if it might be his father calling to apologize, but he knew that was unlikely. His dad was off somewhere drinking beer and feeling bad about what he'd said, but that didn't mean he would think to pick up the phone. Not many people called his number. He considered getting rid of the answering machine, but it had been something that Mary had insisted on having.

He lingered in the tub until all of the heat dissipated, and by the time he decided to dry off, the last light of day had faded from the sky and the coolness of evening had begun. He took his last clean pair of jeans and shirt from the closet. He needed to do laundry, but hadn't been able to force himself to take the dirty clothes to town. It was a task they had done together, a domestic chore they had shared and would now seem too reminiscent of her for him to undertake alone.

In the closet was his only pair of clean boots; he took them to the bed, sitting them on the floor as he grabbed a pair of socks from the drawer. The blinking light of the answering machine caught his eye, and he pushed the button to play the recording. Following the beep was the sound of highway noise. No voice spoke, just the passing sounds of trucks and automobiles. It continued for a few seconds, enough time for his mind to imagine the truck stop at the top of the mountain, or the rest area out on the interstate. Then a car door slammed, its muffled reverberation followed by the drone of a disconnected phone line. He sat on the edge of the bed and pulled on the socks, wondering who it might have been, hoping it had been her.

Grady lived at the foot of the mountain. His house was set back off of the highway and the property was dotted with chicken houses and outbuildings. Pulling into the driveway, Kylmer could see him waiting on the porch, a single yellow bulb illuminating the front of the house, bathing the yard in an unnatural glow. Grady was sitting on the porch rail, talking into a portable phone as Kylmer walked up. Grady gave a quick jerk of his chin by way of greeting and continued his conversation.

"Yeah, my boy'll be there…. Twenty-four hours…right." When he finished Grady hung up. He looked to where Kylmer stood in the yard and grinned.

"Hey, brother man. I haven't seen you around in a while. You look like you've not been eating much. You're getting scrawny. You want me to fix you something?"

Kylmer had no interest in food and answered, "No thanks. I already ate."

They talked for a few minutes before Grady acknowledged the reason for Kyle being there.

"I asked you to come over here because I need some help. Tomorrow evening I have to go down to Charlotte on some business, and I need for you to deliver a car for me. I need you to drive one car up to Virginia and bring another car back down here. Do you think you'll be able to help me out?"

Kylmer knew what this was about and was not against making some easy money.

"Yeah," he said, "I can do that."

Grady got up from the porch rail and started down the steps to the yard.

"That's great. Come out here with me and I'll show you the car."

Kylmer followed him across the yard to a chicken house. The inside of the long building was filled with small birds, covering the dirt floor in a sea of yellow and white.

Near the open door was a white automobile. Chicks were swarming around the tires; they had to kick them out of their way as they entered the building. Large lamps hung from the ceiling, bathing the scurrying birds in harsh light, effecting in the room a sickly yellow pall. The thick air inside of the building was a stifling combination of chicken feed and shit that took Kylmer's breath away, and for a moment made the cold chicken in his stomach turn.

"There's the car I want you to drive up there. Take these." Grady handed him the keys as he moved through the birds towards a control box on the wall.

"I've got to make sure the timer is set so they get food and water tomorrow while I'm away." He began to program the timer, and

Kylmer looked around at all of the birds. They moved in waves from one side of the house to the other. When he began to walk towards the car he noticed that the floor was covered with a line of mashed chicks, just the width of a car tire.

"God almighty, Grady, did you just drive over them on the way in?"

Without looking around from his task Grady said, "Hell yeah, man, you're going to have to do the same. Don't worry about it, though, they're only seven cents apiece."

Kylmer waded through the chickens on his exit to the doors. He wanted to get out of the hot building and breathe air that didn't feel heavy with feathers and dried chickenshit. He hadn't thought much about the car and what it might contain, but he knew that Grady would tell him the important details. The night air was damp and cool, a welcome change from the confines of the chicken house. The evening was clear, and beyond the trees surrounding the yard, he could see the outline of the Blue Ridge. He waited until Grady was finished with his work inside the building, and for the first time felt nervous about being there. He and Grady were almost like kin. Their fathers had both been bootleggers, but only Grady had carried on the family tradition. Kylmer knew that the property, buildings, and chickens were all purchased with cash. He also knew that the car he was going to deliver would be carrying the stuff that earned Grady money, and that he was being asked to drive it because he could be trusted. Kylmer felt duty-bound by history.

"Hey man, here's the deal on the car." Grady offered Kylmer a cigarette, but he refused. "You're going to come by here tomorrow evening at nine o'clock, OK? Drive this rental car up Highway 89 until you get to the top of the mountain. You know that overlook there just past Miller's Tavern?"

Kylmer knew the place; he'd been to the turnoff many times before. His father liked to park his truck there and sit for hours drinking beer. The precipice offered a sweeping view of the valley below. On exceptionally clear days the distant buildings of Piedmont cities could be seen on the horizon. His father had told him a story about it, but he could not remember what he called the place.

Back when only a logging road traversed the mountain, people would stop their wagons at the flat spot overlooking the valley. The story held that a young woman had become pregnant out of wedlock. He was ambitious and she was poor.

"I guess he was the kind of guy that wanted more out of life than could be had around here," his father had said.

"A hillside farm and a house full of kids don't work for everybody," he'd said.

One Sunday afternoon they had gone for a ride in his Surrey, dressed in clothes they could have worn on their wedding day. Her family thought they might be planning to elope, and were not too worried when they stayed gone. It was dark by the time he returned alone, telling of the girl's fall from the overlook. A group of men went out in the night to investigate, and in the purple light of morning, found her body at the bottom of the mountain. Soon after the young man moved away and his name was forgotten to the people of the area, but the story went that on certain nights when the winds lifted up from the valley floor, the cries of the girl and her unborn baby could still be heard.

"There'll be another car just like this one waiting for you." Grady lit a cigarette. "There will be a guy there, a brother from Virginia."

"A brother?"

"Yeah, a black guy. These jigs from up north are trying to get set up. They have some people in Galax and this is my way of showing them who can deliver around here. When you pull in, park a few places away from him. Wait until he gets out and approaches your car. When you see him start towards you, get out. He'll hand you an envelope. All you have to do is take it, get in the car he was driving, and bring it back here. Then go home and wait for me to call you. Got it?"

Kylmer considered the directions for a moment, and Grady finished smoking his cigarette before asking again if there were any questions.

"What if the guy doesn't show?"

"Oh, he'll show up," Grady said, flicking the spent butt into the yard, "this is a big deal for his posse."

"How much money is he supposed to bring?"

"A lot. That's all you need to know."

Kylmer wasn't interested in getting involved in any kind of scene that included guns, so he asked, "What if he tries to fuck me over?"

"If he does, I'll settle up with him. You just get that car back here. Park it in the building and padlock the door behind you when you leave. I'll be in touch with you when I get back from Charlotte, and I'll make it worth your time." Grady looked him over and grinned, his teeth gapped like his sister's. "Maybe you can take a nice vacation. Go out to Utah or wherever and find you some real good shit for your collection."

They walked over to Kylmer's car and stood for a moment, the two of them looking at the night sky. He thought about asking Grady again if he knew anything about Mary, but decided not to bring it up a second time.

"Well, I better be going. I've got to get up early and finish my digging."

"How can you do that shit? Digging around for broken pieces of pottery and junk?"

"I don't think of it like that. I just like finding things, appreciating the past, you know?"

Grady looked at him sideways before feigning a punch to his shoulder.

"You take care of business and be up there before 9:30. Got it?"

Arriving at his dig the next morning, Kylmer immediately noticed that things were not as they had been left. Discarded beer cans were scattered around. The big hole had been uncovered, exposing his shovel and other tools. The brown tarp and bamboo that had concealed the dig were removed and cast aside, the clay floor scarred by lug-soled boot prints. A pile of human stool mounded in the center, but no further digging had taken place there. The damage was done to the two sites he had staked out but not yet excavated. Small hills of dirt stood next to each gaping crater. He inspected the hasty work of those who had ravaged the site in the dark. He didn't even consider the artifacts that might have been taken; instead he picked up the pieces of what had been left behind.

The first bones he came to were leg bones, long and heavy. He was surprised they had retained their density after hundreds of years in the soil. The people who looted the site had tossed them carelessly onto the heaps of dirt. Bewildered by the number of bones littering the area, he began to stack them at the edge of the grave. Some of the smaller ones had been covered by dirt as the looters had continued to dig deeper in the ground in their search for valuables. Kylmer was angry that someone had defiled the site in that way. Ripping up the grave to get a handful of arrowheads. It lacked all respect, to leave human remains cast aside. It made him ashamed to admit that he had left clues that had encouraged them, and that his own excavations were hardly more respectable.

The only thing he could do was rebury the remains. He lay the long ones in the uneven bottoms of the pits and began filling the holes with the dirt. He continued his task until he found the first skull. He stopped to examine it. The other bones could have been dismissed as those of an animal, but the skull was positive proof of the humanity of the site. He imagined there must have been some ceremony when the dead were placed in the ground, so he tried to be solemn in his work of undoing the tresspassers' thoughtless exhumation. There were five in all. Brown-stained craniums long hidden in the earth. Three of the skulls were mature, and the remaining two small. None of them had jaws attached, and only one of the children's skulls was without cracks and holes. He used his finger to trace the orbit of the sockets, cleaning soil from the surface. He noticed that the number of body parts seemed to amount to more than five skulls, and he figured the looters had taken some with them.

He was spooked as he continued the work. The presence of the ones who had previously been there lingered. He recalled Mary's admonition about risk and reward, and he didn't want to imagine the penalty he'd receive if found standing amidst the bones. He tried to conjure soothing images as he wiped sweat from his eyes, but none would come. He could not escape the sensation of being watched. Whether by human eyes hiding in the underbrush of mountain laurel, or the hollow gaze of the eyeless sockets from the skulls, he could not decide. He pictured Mary's bulging eyelids as she lay in restful repose on their bed. He heard her voice in his head, but nothing she said gave him ease.

She always called him by his full name, as if he were to be confused with someone else in her mind.

"Why do you care, Kylmer Hayes," she said when he asked when she last had her period. "You might gonna be a daddy? Is that what you're worried about, baby? Don't you fret about that none," she said, and laughed as she walked out of the room. He only knew of one reason a woman would not have her period, and he wanted to know if he were responsible for it. She never gave him an answer and he was left to ponder it still. She packed up some of her things that night and took off.

The next morning Kylmer left for the canyon lands of the Four Corners region. He'd been promised a good payday for helping a man dig pots from ruins of an ancient cliff dwelling. Each one would be sold for several thousand dollars, and the risks associated with their retrieval were equally exorbitant. It was the opportunity of a lifetime, he'd thought.

They had used burros to haul a pneumatic drill and generator into the isolated canyon. There they had cut pictographs from cave walls. A wealthy collector had paid a great deal of money to have the museum quality images, and Kylmer had been rewarded handsomely. The cliff dwellings hid a treasure of things left where they had been abandoned centuries before. Fiber sandals lay next to bowls of corn; cooking utensils, half covered in dust, remained where they had been left alongside finely crafted pots and bowls resting in their ancient storage places. It had proven to be a remarkable cache, a place he had only dreamed of ever finding, but the experience affected him in an unexpected way. He began to feel like an interloper, ashamed for disrupting time suspended. The trip was the first time he had felt embarrassed by what he did to make money.

On a rock ledge at the back of the cave they had found a bundle of skins. Wrapped inside was the corpse of an infant, perfectly preserved by the arid climate. His partner had wanted to take it with them, knowing it was invaluable to wealthy collectors, but Kylmer had angrily resisted. They had taken enough from the site, he protested. Where beautiful pots and bowls had remained undisturbed for hundreds of years, were now gaping holes. Where ancient hands had drawn precious images on the cliff walls, were left ragged wounds of the drill. Unable to sleep that last night, Kylmer lay listening to the night sounds of the canyon floor below.

Before leaving the cave the next morning, he took time to shovel dirt into the pocked places where the artifacts had been removed. He traced the holes in the cliff wall with his hands and felt enormous regret for what he was doing. As his companion packed the burros,

Kylmer made certain the infant corpse remained on the ledge where it had been found. Taking a final accounting of their work, he was convinced that more had been disturbed than could ever be undone.

Now, several weeks later, standing amidst the half-buried bones, he felt again the same haunted sensation of his final moments spent in the cave. He remembered that Mary had come back the day after his return, paler than before and seeming to have more to keep to herself. They never talked of where she had been, or if she were carrying a baby; all that mattered was that she had returned. He hoped that it meant they would make a life together and she would stop smoking cocaine and running around, and if there were a baby, he'd take care of it. It would mean that she found in him a future worth having.

It took a couple of hours to re-inter the remains, but he was able to leave the graves looking almost undisturbed. Only a keen eye would have noticed the different colored soil on the surface, but he knew that would quickly disappear. The most obvious sign would be the slight indentation that occurred after the soil settled and com- pacted. Most of the day was gone by the time he began filling the big hole. Layer by layer he had meticulously exposed the stratums of history, finding in each level more rare artifacts. It had been several days' work with the promise of more yet to uncover, but he began filling the hole anyway. It took the rest of the afternoon to finish the job, and by the time he was through, the sun had disappeared behind the trees. He packed his tools and began the brief hike to the car. He stopped before cresting the ridge and looked back on the place and vowed to never come there again.

There were no messages on the answering machine, and no sign that she had been there. He thought about taking a bath before going to Grady's, but he had no clean clothes to put on and decided to lie on the couch and rest for a while. He had three hours before he needed to leave the house, and he figured that he would be awake in plenty of time to freshen up before leaving. The front room of the house was cool and dark, and he drifted into a restless sleep.

Dreams came to him. He saw his father and Mary. The two of them, sitting in a horse-drawn buggy high on a hill, motioning for him to come up and join them. His father was smiling, dressed in the suit he wore to church when he was still young. Mary's hair was long and moving in the wind. She wore a blue dress and when she stood; he could see her long legs silhouetted through the fabric. She motioned for him to join them, but the hill was too steep for him to climb. He kept trying to scramble up to them, but made no progress in his efforts. Eventually they stopped beckoning to him and began using their hands to dig in the earth. The dirt they removed cascaded down the hill to where he stood. As they disappeared beneath the surface, other objects began tumbling down the hillside. Chicken carcasses, skulls and beer cans. Precious artifacts he had never seen the like of, lances and breast plates, painted vessels and garments adorned with shells and feathers. He heard faint moans coming from inside the hill. The volume building, culminating in a crescendo of howls. A thousand voices calling to him from the earth.

He awakened to the ringing of the phone, but couldn't clear his head from the dream in time to answer it. When he got to the bedside table, the machine had picked up and a busy signal was sounding through the tinny speaker. He looked at the clock and went straight away to the bathroom to wash his face. It was past 8:30. He would need close to thirty minutes to get from where he was to where he had to be.

He drove away from the house into a nether land where dreams intersect reality. Even though he rode with the windows down, he had to fight sleep and the temptation to return to the other consciousness where she had been. It took several miles before he emerged from the clouded perception. He parked the car in front of Grady's and proceeded immediately to the chicken house. Entering the brightly-lit building, once again he felt overwhelmed by the smell of the birds.

They hadn't discussed the particulars of getting the car out of the building, but Kylmer saw no other option than to open both doors and back the car out into the night. He thought of the birds escaping, but remembered that Grady had not placed much value on the ones he had run over. He left the doors opened and marveled that none of the small chickens rushed to liberate themselves from the confines of the room. He didn't bother to clear a path on his way to the car, steeling himself for the moment when many would be crushed by the car tires. The chickens moved as if one to the opposite end of the building with the start of the engine. He backed the car out and stopped to close the doors before continuing on to his destination.

The rental car had a peculiar scent, a combination of new car smell and the pungent aroma of the packaged marijuana in the trunk. In the passenger seat was a pack of cigarettes Grady had left. He turned onto the paved road, checking the time of the dashboard clock. He had fifteen minutes to make the overlook, which was cutting it close. The patched road to the mountain was a narrow two-lane that wound its way through the foothills past fruit orchards and tobacco fields, not a route to make up lost time by.

The road began its curving ascent up the mountainside, and Kylmer went over again the procedure laid out by Grady. He wanted to finish this business quickly and return home without any complications. The tavern that his father frequented was just up ahead and he saw his truck sitting out front. The dreamed image of his father dressed in Sunday clothes was still vivid in his mind. For a moment, he tried to remember why they had stopped going to church, why they ever went in the first place. It didn't matter much anymore, he decided. His father had found other ways to ease the guilt he felt about things he could not undo.

Kylmer imagined what the climb up the mountain would have been like in the days before paved roads and automobiles. A trek that now took only a few minutes would have taken hours in a horse-drawn wagon, he concluded. The gray hardtop of the road gave way to fresh black asphalt as he crossed the state line and entered the steepest curves of the journey, signaling the approach of his destination. He recalled the vision of his father and Mary sitting in the buggy, smiling down at him and he knew he should be thinking of more immediate things. The final few curves were sharp and narrow and Kylmer was careful to prepare for the left-hand turn into the parking area of the scenic overlook.

The parking area was fairly wide, and all of the trees had been cleared from around the asphalt, creating the illusion of being suspended in the night's sky. He saw the waiting car as he slowed to turn off of the highway. The driver had backed into a space, and Kylmer Hayes' headlights swept the area, illuminating, for a brief moment, a pale female face in the passenger's seat. He pulled into a parking space a few yards away from the driver's side. Before he could set the brake, the people were out of the other car and the driver was walking towards him. Kylmer left the engine running and breathed in the car's heavy funk before opening the door to stand up. It was a dark night, no moon illuminated the mountain, and only a few dim stars shone in the sky. He could barely make out the features of the approaching figure, but he could see thick braids of hair sprouting from his head, tied in a bunch. The woman had disappeared from Kylmer's peripheral vision, so he focused on the black male standing in front of him.

The man said, "Tell your boy Grady I'll be talking to him, and make sure he gets this," then handed Kylmer a large envelope. He felt compelled to look around and locate the woman, but decided it would be better to go directly to the other car before someone else pulled into the parking area. As he approached the car, he heard two doors close behind him. He turned around and watched them drive away. He leaned towards the car, straining to make out the features of the female passenger gazing back at him, briefly illuminated in the red glow of the brake lights. Squinting in vain he watched the taillights disappear around the curve leading over the crest of the mountain. He stood for a moment looking out into the purple void of the night sky and down to the valley below. A few lonely lights shimmered in the distance. The solitude of the place was intensified by the wind blowing down from the mountaintop and, for the first time since his aborted dream, he felt fully awake. The sound of an engine laboring up the winding road reminded him of what was left to do.

He dropped the envelope in the passenger's seat and started the engine. The smell of the car was familiar, but dissimilar to the one he had been driving. The newness of the car was enhanced by a subtle scent, an intimate smell. It was not a perfume, but the essence of a female. Lights appeared as a truck turned into the overlook. He turned away from the headlights and waited until the driver had parked before pulling away. He drove down the mountain trying to keep his mind clear. He did not want to think about his own circumstances, or his father's story about the girl and the baby. As he passed the tavern at the foot of the mountain, he didn't bother to look for his father's truck in the parking lot. He didn't want to think about him either. He wanted only to have it done and return to the house where sleep awaited him. He rolled down the windows, inviting the cool air to erase the vexing smell and cleanse his senses.

He dreaded reentering the chicken house, but found it easier to drive through the birds the second time. The small birds popped in muffled explosions as the tires plowed through their wake, and when he applied the brakes, the car slid to a slow halt. He picked up the envelope from the passenger's seat thinking to place it behind the visor as Grady had instructed. There on the seat was the clay pipe he thought had been misplaced. In that moment he realized what had happened, and held his breath as he confronted what he had hoped to deny. Like a slap, his cheeks stung, and in an effort to unburden himself, he exhaled the air in his lungs loudly. Kylmer left the pipe on the seat and covered it again with the envelope. He paused to look at his reflection in the car's window for an extended moment, then began closing and padlocking the doors to the building.

The short drive to his house allowed time enough for him to decide what needed to be done. He would take the dirty clothes into town the next morning and go to the laundry mat. He would discard all the things that reminded him of her, and purge himself of ghosts from the past. He didn't care if every grave in the river bottom was looted; it was all there for the taking and he'd plundered more than his share. He was done with it all. He thought about the dream, his father in the suit and Mary with her long hair. He wondered if there was a baby, and if so what would become of it now.

Kylmer Hayes pulled into the yard and sat looking at the darkened house. It wasn't the same place he had left. The dead bushes loomed from the shadows, mocking his best intentions. He took his shovel from the bed of the truck, and walked to where the lifeless bushes were. He didn't need to dig the earth from around their base. The plants had never taken root in the red earth below the eves of the house, and he effortlessly dislodged them from the ground with the first tug of the clumped branches. He ripped them all from their place and piled them at the edge of the fallow garden. He tore the useless wooden stakes from ground where they supported large clumps of brittle pole beans and shriveled tomato plants, and stacked them and stunted corn stalks on top of the bushes, making a pile of the uncultivated crops. Kylmer doused the mound with kerosene, then entered the house to look for something to light it with.

He remembered that Mary had kept a lighter in the drawer next to the bedside table, and went to retrieve it from the dark room. The answering machine sat atop the table, the red light flashing. Kylmer opened the drawer and fumbled in the dark until he felt the lighter. He put it in his pocket, then picked up the answering machine, jerking the cords from the jacks in the wall. He carried the appliance she had insisted on having out to the yard and cast it onto the pile of brush. Next, he dragged from the house the headboard of the bed they slept on and added it to the pile. He continued reentering the house until he had cleared it of everything he could remember her touching, adding it all to the growing heap of things he wanted to be rid of.

He returned to the room they shared and took from the closet the few clothes she'd left behind. He folded them neatly, then rolled them into tight bundles. He stuffed them into the large Anasazi pots he kept hidden in the back of the closet, the ones that he'd thought were going to provide her with the things she needed. He cleared the bathroom of her cosmetics and toothbrush and added them to the pots, and carried them out to the porch. He picked up the shovel from the yard and walked to the back of the house. He chose a place near the edge of the yard, where the grass gave way to woods. He began to dig and soon was perspiring in the cool evening air. He made the hole plenty deep and wide, then went to fetch the pots. He placed them in the ground and unceremoniously covered them with foreign soil.

Kylmer lit the pyre and stood back to watch it burn. Thick smoke carried away pieces of the past that he wished gone, and long red flames lapped at the night's sky above the tin-roofed house. He stayed there until the fire had almost died before reentering the emptied rooms.

He was left with what he had found. Items she had never held or shown any appreciation of, things that would not burn anyway. He picked up the pipe and held it as he lay back on the floor. In the darkened room he fingered the face carved in stone, caressing the relief of the features. Before falling into sleep he thought about his father sitting in his pickup at the overlook, and he remembered what he had called the place.

Wade was down on his luck when Marlow offered him the job. He'd been working at a package store since the furniture factory shut down. His wife had divorced him, gotten a breast enhancement, moved in with a younger man. He turned forty-five a few days before Marlow called.

The first thing his former partner said was, "Wade you ain't too old and fat to climb, are you?" Then, "I have an opportunity I'd like to discuss with you." They agreed to meet at a bar; Marlow would buy him a few beers.

At the bar, Marlow took the lid off one end of a cardboard tube, and pulled out a rolled document. He moved bottles out of the way, dried the counter with bar napkins, and unfurled a map in front of Wade. Spread on the bar was a satellite photograph of the United States, the border of each state highlighted in yellow. Across the map were clusters of different colored dots-blue, red, and white.

Marlow wiped his hand across the photograph, as if clearing it for better viewing.

"You know what this is?" he asked tapping the center of the picture.

"Kansas?" Wade responded.

"No smart ass, the dots." Marlow lit a cigarette, placed the ashtray at one corner of the photo, holding down the curled edge. "Every one of them colored dots is a transmission tower, cell tower, radio tower, microwave tower. The different colors represent the height. Blue is under five hundred feet, red up to a thousand, white the tallest ones."

Wade listened while Marlow explained how he'd won a bid to paint towers. The jobs were out west and he needed someone he could trust to lead one of two crews.

Wade noticed Marlow had gotten too fat to climb towers. A

steady diet of caffeine and nicotine kept Wade thin. Standing from the stool, Marlow's belly strained against the buttons of his shirt, and teetering on pointed toed cowboy boots, Wade thought how he looked kind of like a penguin. Then he asked Wade a question.

"You still do any bird hunting?"

"Nah, I gave it up after my dad died. I got to where it kind of bothered me to kill them."

"What do you mean?"

"It made me sick to see 'em fall. You know how they buckle in the air and fall spinning? I just couldn't do it anymore."

Marlow dropped a twenty on the bar, patted Wade on the back. "Alright big shot, I'll be in touch."

In the fifteen years since Wade and Marlow worked together, Marlow had gone on to build the business. As younger men, they made money painting things no one else would consider; water towers, bridges, storage tanks, anything too tall. Wade had never been afraid of heights, but after a couple of years painting water towers, he got to where he couldn't sleep at night. He'd startle awake from dreams of falling. In the dreams his body was heavy and the ground raced up to meet him as he hurtled downward, gravity pulling at him, drawing him downward in a rapid vortex. His wife told him how he'd holler and flail around. Wade knew he screamed out; it was as if yelling might stop his fall. His wife said that if you didn't wake before hitting the ground, you'd die in your sleep. But how could anyone know that?

After he quit climbing and painting, Wade took a job at the furniture factory. It didn't pay as well, but gluing maple veneer on cabinets was a lot safer. After a while he stopped dreaming of falling, and counted on working at the factory until he retired. That had been the plan.

Wade took a couple of days to consider Marlow's offer. He knew it might be his only last chance to make a decent pay check. There weren't any manufacturing jobs around. He figured that by the fall he'd have to sell his house and split the money with his ex-wife. Maybe he could combine that money with what he'd earn painting and buy the package store. It wasn't much of a scheme, but it was all he could come up with. He called Marlow three days after their meeting, and agreed to work the summer; they'd have to wait and see about anything more after that.

Before they left for the Great Plains, Marlow hosted a barbecue for all the workers. Marlow had also hired another old partner to lead one of the two crews. Slawter's gang consisted of Darren and Derrick, twin brothers with red hair and fair skin, looking like they would toast in the summer sun. There was a college kid with long matted hair called Toad. Two other hippie looking college boys, Keith and Chance joined Joey, a recent high school graduate in Wade's crew. The Mexican kid, Angel Ramirez would switch-off with each crew. Wade wondered where Marlow found this bunch of dead beats, but he kept it to himself.

They drank beer from a keg, and ate pork shoulders before the boss laid down the ground rules.

"Alright fellas. Now, you young guys need to know a couple of things. You're representing me. I won't allow no drinking on the job, no drugging, and whoring at night. I can't have my vans getting cracked up, or the equipment busted. I can't afford to have nobody getting hurt. That would mess things up for all of us. Are you with me?"

Marlow looked at the workers for a moment, before continuing.

"Wade and Slawter are in charge, and they don't have to put up with any bullshit. I'm going to check in with them each evening, and if there are any problems, I'm buying a bus ticket home for you, and it is coming out of your paycheck. Anybody have a problem with that? There isn't going to be much time for screwing around. You work till you finish a job, and then pack it up and head on to the next." Marlow made it clear that this was an important contract, and that if things went well, there could be more work for everyone.

After the younger guys left, Marlow handed Slawter and Wade a company credit card, and cell phone.

"Pay for all expenses with the card, and I'll check in with you guys every day," he said. Then he wished them luck and told them to be safe.

The three longhaired college boys rode in the van with Wade. They'd brought repelling ropes, and other gear they used for rock climbing, told Wade they planned to use it for work. The first day driving, they listened to cassette tapes the boys had brought. Live recordings of Grateful Dead shows, songs lasting for thirty miles, and more. Wade didn't mind the music, but the second day, somewhere west of St. Louis; he learned how wide the gap between them would be.

The boys were talking about a concert coming up in August, an outdoor show in Colorado. As they discussed girlfriends, and the concert, Wade recognized a song on the tape. It was a cover version of "Mama Tried."

"Hey fellas," Wade said. "That's a Merle Haggard song," he told them.

"Nah, man," one responded. "That's Jerry Garcia."

From then on Wade referred to all three as *hey Deadhead*, and he asked if they had any other tapes to play. They did, but they all sounded the same.

The third day, before crossing into Wyoming, they stopped at a truck stop. When the Deadheads got back in the van, they reeked of pot. Wade decided not to mention it. He and Marlow used to get stoned when they worked together, and it hadn't been a big deal. He still liked to light up on occasion. Wade would be cool about it, as long as they were busy and not acting stupid.

Once the jobs began, Wade realized how much he missed working outside. He enjoyed the unfamiliar geography around him. Unlike the foothills he was accustomed to, the plains and open sky created a grandness of scale that made him feel small, especially when he climbed the heights of the towers. In the distance, the western horizon gave way to mountains rising abruptly from the flat land, like jagged teeth. The surroundings were foreign to him, and exciting, a thrill he kept to himself.

The towers were always located in removed places where wildlife appeared in abundance. The field glasses he used to keep up with the painters high on the tower were just as often used to survey the animals in the distance. He'd never seen a pronghorn antelope until Gillette, Wyoming. Sand hill cranes, bigger than herons, stalked the shallows of the North Platte River, and birds following an ingrained migratory path, heading south.

It was work more fit for younger men's bodies. Even though Wade was thin and fit for a forty-five-year-old man, the climbing part was tiring. Some mornings, on the tallest towers when they had to go all the way to the top, the day started with an ascent of more than an hour. On those dark mornings, Wade hooked his safety harness onto the cable and mounted the rungs with sore knees. He made steady progress, silently working his way to the glowing beacon at the tip of the structure.

Wade enjoyed climbing half-way up the tower and sitting on one of the work platforms, smoking a cigarette and admiring the land below and beyond. There were times when, if he looked to the sky, the movement of clouds and the subtle sway of the tower made him feel the sensation of vertigo. He learned to overcome the feeling by looking at the metal structure for a moment; closing his eyes only made it worse.

The younger guys scrambled to the top. Except for one, the young kid named Joey. The other guys began calling him "Slowey" due to the sloth-like pace of his climbing. It was clear to Wade that the boy was terrified, and he knew how that could cause problems. Wade took to climbing behind Joey, hoping it would help him overcome the fear. The boy made it through the first couple of jobs, and then one day in Nebraska he froze.

The tower was only five hundred feet tall, sitting on a bluff overlooking a river. The job had been moving quickly, weather dry and hot. Wade liked the location. The sandbars of the river were a breeding ground for cranes. From the tower, he could see the large white birds wading in the shallows. It was a pleasant scene to look down upon.

The crew was anxious to finish the job. They'd have two days off once it was done. Their first break in over a month. It would be a chance to drink beer, sit around the motel pool before driving on to Colorado. Wade followed Joey up the tower, when he noticed the boy had stopped climbing, his knees shaking.

"What are you doing, Joey?" Wade asked from where they'd stopped, about half-way up.

"I can't move," the kid said.

"Damn boy, you got to move," Wade told him. "Just look straight ahead and keep climbing." But the kid was beyond reason. He started sobbing, snot bubbling out of his nose.

"I can't fucking move," he cried. His legs trembling out of control, arms hugging the girders of the metal structure.

It was times like that when the safety harness made all the difference. Wade had to stay with him, talk sense to him, and explain that he was in a safety harness and couldn't possibly fall. It took thirty minutes to get the kid to calm down, or about as long as it would have taken them to make it the rest of the way up the tower. When he calmed down to just quivering, the only direction the kid was going was back down.

Wade had no choice but descend with him, costing half a day of work, setting the crew back. The boy stayed in the van the rest of the time. They put him on a bus back home when they got into town, and the crew headed for Colorado short-handed. It was just the start of guys giving up on the project.

They'd made good time the first few weeks, finishing twice as many towers in the time Marlow had scheduled. It put them ahead, so Marlow bid six more jobs, in Kansas and Oklahoma. After Joey left, Angel joined Wade's crew. The Deadheads were working fast; at the end of the day they repelled down the side of the towers, descending like spiders. Their quick drop saved an hour each day, it added up. Slawter's crew kept pace. It had been going well until Marlow wired paychecks to Colorado.

They'd worked four jobs east of the Front Range. The flat lands were still green from spring rains, and the towers they painted were set in the middle of free range cattle land. When Marlow wired the money to a bank in Ft. Collins, Slawter and Wade passed out the checks to the members of each crew. It was the last they saw of the college boys. They took their money and repelling ropes and headed for Boulder, to the girls and concert Wade had heard them talking about.

Then it was down to a single five-man crew. Slawter and Wade forced to do more climbing. Angel and the twins painted long hours, stayed busy, and they made it to Oklahoma by September. Then things slowed down. They were preparing to paint a tower south of Ardmore when a cold front moved through bringing rain. It kept them off the job for two days. The twins got a call from Marlow; their mother had died. They headed back to North Carolina, and it was down to three to finish the final four towers Marlow had contracted. They had four weeks to pull it off. That is when they started riding the line.

To make the job move faster, the first thing they did at each tower was to fix the rigging at the top. Slawter climbed to the summit attached a boom with a pulley, while Wade set-up the wench and prepared the generator. Once everything was secured at the top, Slawter would feed the rope down, a five-gallon bucket of paint serving as ballast. They started hauling themselves to the top, riding the line. Wade suspected the OSHA people wouldn't approve, the line was only intended to carry equipment, but it was a new industry, and you did what you had to do.

Wade didn't mind going first. Once the safety harness was hooked to the rope, it was kind of like a ride at the amusement park. In the dark of morning, he leaned back and looked at the red light atop the tower, blinking as the wench dragged him to the boom near the top. Every few hundred feet, the pulley rope hit a place where the lengths had been spliced together. As the thickened part of the line passed over the wheel of the pulley, there was a lurch. A sickening second where the harness jerked, and the sensation of weightlessness making his insides float, like a roller-coaster, but with a lot more reason to be scared.

They used a radio to communicate; when to slow the pulley, how close the rider was to approaching the stopping place. The way the rig worked, Wade was just a couple of feet outside the metal girders, and could easily reach out and grab the tower when it came time to crawl inside, detach from the rope, and hook on to the safety cable within the structure. It saved a couple of hours each day, but meant that only two could ride, the other had to run the wench, and climb later. It was the only way that three men could finish the jobs already agreed to.

They made it to Texas before Slawter quit. Painting a radio transmission tower east of Denton was the last job before heading back to North Carolina. It was the tallest one yet, more than one thousand-four hundred feet, and they'd already gotten the rigging in place when Slawter's wife told him something that made him return home.

Wade overheard part of the phone conversation before leaving the motel room.

"Goddamn Lisa, I done give you every cent I earn. What more do you want?" Slawter said. When Wade came back to the room, Slawter was packing his stuff in one of the two vans. Wade watched him drive away; he then called Marlow to tell him what had happened. It was just Wade and the Mexican kid left to finish a job that needed four men, three at the very least.

Wade was sprawled on the motel bed waiting for Marlow to call back, half watching a golf match on the television. The commentators were telling how one of the golfers had overcome "the yips." Replays showed the man going through a prolonged ritual. He wiggled his ass, wagged the club head around the ball, digging the spikes of his shoes into the turf, taking forever. *Just hit the damn thing*, Wade felt like saying. How hard could it be? It wasn't a life or death decision. He knew guys who had frozen on the job, couldn't go through with their duties, but that was a whole different thing from going psycho over a fucking golf ball.

But there it was, this golfer wiggling his ass around with the yips. "What a fucking joke," Wade said just as Angel came back into the room. He liked the kid. He kept quiet, worked hard, never seemed to mind that the guys on the crew called him Pedro. They called him that before they all quit.

"Wade, I'm in a bind," Marlow said when he called. "If you guys can't finish it up fast, I'll lose another contract."

Wade knew it was going to be tough to do, just him and the kid.

"I can't promise anything," he told Marlow. "We'll try."

"You get it done, and there will be a fat bonus. I'll give you the wages those other assholes would've earned. Maybe you can buy that package store," Marlow said.

They'd slept in the van for two nights, working after dark in the full moon, the job almost finished. The last thing to do was disassemble the aluminum workstations spaced equally, dividing the tower in thirds. Once they were lowered to the ground, they could head home and collect their bonus. Air conditioned days at the package store occupied Wade's thoughts in those last long hours of work.

The way he'd decided to finish the job, Angel would run the wench, and Wade would ride the line, send the equipment back down where Angel would load it into the van. It should be quick work, and they could be done before the weather turned ugly, another cold front was headed south, and rain and high winds were called for. Not weather for climbing towers. Plus, they had two days to be off the site, and Marlow had promised a bonus if they got done before the deadline.

The last night they slept amid the equipment in the back of the van. Sometime in the night, Wade awoke to the sound of things falling on the van's metal roof. It wasn't the ping of hail, but a more substantive thud; ten, twelve times it happened before Wade decided to look out the window. Even with a mostly full moon beaming through the gathering clouds, he saw nothing except the glow of lights attached to the tower and the thick guy wires stretching in the distance. Angel slept through the noise, but Wade couldn't get back to sleep.

He left the van, lit a cigarette, and took a couple of steps before kicking the first bird. He picked up a limp necked duck, and looked around at the shadowy lumps littering the ground around the van. Walking the perimeter of the tower, there were hundreds of ducks, geese, starlings, a few still twitching, wings fanned on the dewy grass. Wade looked up to the tower, a thickening fog hiding the top, the guy wires disappearing into the clouds, maybe half the tower enshrouded, the cloud cover swelling red with the glow of the lights hidden above.

He roused Angel, told him to be ready, that the weather wasn't going to hold. It was still a couple of hours from dawn, the autumn days growing shorter.

Wade filled the generator with gasoline, checked the oil, made sure things were squared away on the ground. He thought about the birds, their bodies surrounding the tower. He remembered the days when he enjoyed killing ducks, and why he'd stopped.

Maybe the clouds had blinded them. Did the glowing lights draw them to their death, crashing into the tower? Had they circled the structure, only to be cut down by the guy wires? It was a strange thing to be in the midst of and made him uneasy. Spooked, he cranked the generator, let it idle while Angel set-up a work light and checked the radio batteries. Wade decided not to mention the birds unless the kid brought it up. He figured that the morning light would make it obvious, and there was no need to start the day with talk of things fallen to the ground.

"All right, let's do it," he finally said.

"As I'm riding to the top, remember to go slow, I'll let you know when I'm getting close, and you just back off of it a little at a time. Got it?" Wade trusted the kid, and thought how he'd kind of miss him once the job was over. The kid nodded.

Angel helped Wade hook his harness to the hitch, went to the wench and waited for Wade to give the thumbs up before engaging the levers that would hoist him to the top. Wade leaned back, tested the tension of the rope before giving the signal to start the pulley. Angel engaged the wench slowly, and Wade's feet lifted off the ground as he looked to the sky, the clouds hiding his destination.

Wade did something he rarely ever did; he looked back over his shoulder to the ground. The work light illuminated the area where Angel tended the wench, the hum of the generator becoming fainter as the rope dragged him toward the top. He felt the first hitch in the rope, his stomach and balls feeling the familiar weightless sensation. He thought he'd wait to check the radio, make sure Angel had his turned on. Then the radio barked.

"How's the ride?" Angel asked.

"Smooth," Wade responded.

"I can't see you anymore, you are in heaven," Angel said.

Wade wondered if there were more birds coming that way, and he hoped not to get popped by a flock of them, but that was a silly thought at this time, he knew.

The cloud cover loomed closer, and Wade rode into the flickering gloom, eight hundred feet above earth, the sky damp, holding precipitation. The tower disappeared, the fog swallowing him, a pulsating glow of the shrouded lights above. He could imagine the flock of birds flying head-long into the metal, something that shouldn't be there; a man-made tower blocking their innate migratory patterns. He reached for the radio. He wanted Angel to begin slowing the wench.

The rope hitched again, but it wasn't right. He looked to the heavens, the throb of light somewhere closer, sounds of wind all he could hear. He didn't know if he was still moving. He let go of the radio, not knowing if it fell or rose. The clouds around him swirled in a confusing direction, a sick horror rising, climbing to his chest, his throat.

He couldn't tell which direction he was moving in, or where he was in relation to the tower, but he knew he was weightless, not at all like in the dreams. He heard his own voice, the high pitch of his scream, and he reached, grabbing at the shadows.

Lucky Break

The bartender brought another draft beer, sat it in front of Baine, picked up three dollars from the stack of bills on the counter, and returned with the change. "Thanks," Baine said, lighting another cigarette.

It was a beer joint with pool tables, no windows. A red neon rack and cues advertised the amusements to be found inside. It was the kind of place people go to get drunk. Sitting across the street from boarded up mills, it had seen better days, times when mill-workers stopped in after their shift, back when the clatter of looms earned the neighborhood the name Needle Town. Baine hadn't lived there long, just enough to learn jobs were hard to come by, and that there were places where he might revisit bad habits.

Because banks were closed for Martin Luther King's birthday, the man on the phone asked Baine if he would accept a personal check. That was okay with Baine. Cash would have been a temptation. He might spend it on things he didn't really want, or need. With money in his pocket, he could change his life. He could drive away, and make a new start somewhere else. Men did it all the time.

"A check's okay," Baine told him.

"These guns aren't registered, are they?" he asked Baine. "I'm no thief, it's just I don't like the government telling me what to do." Baine understood. They agreed to meet in a dentist office parking lot where the man had an appointment. "What kind of vehicle will you be driving?" the man asked.

"A old Chevy pickup," Baine replied. "I'll be the guy in dark glasses. The one who looks like he's selling guns in the parking lot of a dentist office." The guy chuckled, told him he'd see him there.

He hated to sell the guns. They were his inheritance. But a few weeks before, his wife came home from work and made it plain. "Damn Baine, you haven't worked since we got here. The car insurance is due, hospital bills. Jarrod's birthday is next week. What in the hell are you going to do about it?"

He sold the motorcycle first thing, then collected the pistols. Sometimes he wished they weren't in the house, he had kids and his wife didn't like guns, but he'd kept them because they meant something to his dad. The one he hated to sell the most was the gun his father had carried in the war. A silver-plated Colt .45; it was a gun that killed Nazis.

"What tunes you want to hear?" a woman at the bar asked him now. He'd noticed her shooting pool when he walked in, thin, short hair with highlights, not bad looking at all. She'd smiled when she came to the bartender for change. Baine smiled back, but just a little. He had enough problems as it was. She wore a fitted denim jacket with an American flag on the back. She was patriotic, he thought. A lot of people were these days. When she bent over to shoot, her jacket rose, exposing the soft flesh of her back, orange and purple wings of a tattooed butterfly at the top of turquoise panties, bright enough to see from across the gloomy room.

"Play your favorite," Baine said over the crack of pool balls. Moving to the jukebox, she looked good walking away. Maybe she had an apartment in town, or lived out in the country in a trailer where they could spend a few hours feeling good, worry about it later. It was quite an assumption, but after several beers he'd abandoned the bleakness of reality.

The check was lying on the bar next to his cigarettes. Her selection began on the jukebox - *Take me down to Paradise City, where the grass is green and the girls are pretty.* The woman took a seat near the end of the bar and leaned across whispering to the bartender. Baine read the address on the check, a pricey neighborhood out on the lake where doctors lived. He knew the guy had money when he arrived at the parking lot. Baine hadn't asked what type of car he would be driving, but when the black Mercedes SUV pulled in, the driver threw up a hand, recognizing Baine sitting in the old truck.

"What year is that?" the guy asked, shaking hands.

"1960," Baine told him. The man's car was worth more than Baine's house. His teeth were immaculate. Baine couldn't imagine why he'd need an appointment with the dentist. The only time Baine went was if there was a problem. Maybe it was to get them polished. His teeth looked like pearls, deep enamel, glinting in the morning sun.

"I'll tell you what I'll do," the man smiled. "I'll hold on to these for a couple of months, you get back on your feet, I'll sell them back for the same price. How's that sound?" Baine shook his hand, put the check in his jacket pocket, said thanks. Two months wouldn't make a difference, but it was decent all the same.

The bartender brought another beer-*Oh won't you please take me home*-the song gaining momentum, and the woman smoked a cigarette, looking at her reflection in the bar back mirror. Baine's stack of bills thinned. He'd lost track of how many he'd had. He lit another cigarette, and considered the possibility of taking off with her. She was watching him in the mirror behind the stacks of beveled glass mugs, jars of pickled eggs, red-hot sausages. He took a deep drag off the cigarette, looked away from her gaze.

Someone opened the door to the bar. Baine noticed it getting dark outside. Time to make a decision. With the cigarette dangling from his lip, he closed one eye to the smoke, finished the beer, and picked up what remained of the money on the counter. He looked at the check the man had written, in the amount of eight hundred dollars.

Baine dropped a five-dollar bill on the counter, stubbed out the cigarette, and slid the check in his pocket, relieved at having something to show for his day, things might be better for a while. In his peripheral vision, the woman turned his way, rotating on the stool, opening herself to him. He nodded to the bartender, zipped the motorcycle jacket to his chin.

Guns 'n Roses roared from the jukebox as he stepped away from the bar. Turning towards the woman he smiled; she cocked her head slightly, bit the corner of her lip. Baine started to say something, but she looked away. It was probably all for the best, he thought. He turned to leave, hoping that the truck would start. He felt certain that outside the bar, in the neon-infused gloaming he'd find comfort in driving the few blocks home, thankful at having one less thing to regret.

The back of the house faced the direction from which weather originated. To the north and west approached the type of storm that came down out of Canada fast, rushing across the plains, spreading like a vapor, catching people off-guard. Living things would die as a result. She'd known a person who froze to death. Her one distinction-she'd known people who died in almost every conceivable way.

She stood at the back door waiting for the dog to finish sniffing around in the lifeless grass and clumps of dead shrubbery. The clouds, off in the distance, bulged like Curtains of cold sheet metal. The bell tower atop the boarded up school, long silent, stood out against the dark sky as if it were still important. The Blue Norther would make it in from the panhandle by afternoon and people would stay indoors. It would be no different than other days for her. The only time she ventured out of the house was when she tended the dog.

Warm in a red sweater, the dog was in no hurry, she knew that when the coldest weather arrived, the dog would be reluctant to go back out in the yard. She patiently stood looking out the glass storm door waiting for the dog to plod its way back to the bottom step. She looked at her watch and realized that it was time to take her morning medication.

"Come on in now, baby, Momma has to take her pills."

The black dog came running up to the back step and she let her into the warm kitchen. She closed the door and locked the series of latches and hooks, first the storm door and then the wooden interior one. The neighborhood had changed in the years since the Railroad closed up shop. From her window she had been witness to the long and steady decline, a transformation that compounded her solitude.

The houses of proud working men abandoned. The color of the houses and people had once been uniformly white. The sounds of the neighborhood, in the past dominated by family activities, were now replaced by the din of loud car stereos, and Spanish, and crudity. She didn't feel safe even though the windows had iron bars, and the doors bolted at top and bottom.

Sitting at the kitchen table she lifted the dog onto her lap where she meticulously washed the animal's paws and made sure that all was clean.

"Momma has to wash that girl, make sure she gets all clean...I gotta take care of my baby."

The dog, a mute partner in the ongoing conversations, a one sided dialogue having no beginning or end.

She placed the dog on the floor and roused herself to make her way across the small kitchen to where the pills and chart were located atop the microwave oven. She did all of her cooking in the microwave, mostly warming up canned food that she had delivered from the grocery store down the street. It had been a long time since she cooked a dinner on her gas stove. She wasn't sure how long it had been exactly, the last time the kids came for a visit, which had been years. The store that made home deliveries was going to close in a few weeks, and she worried how she would get her groceries once that happened. Although she had not driven the car in almost a year, it was still parked out in the building and if a necessity, she could drive to the store. "Baby- Momma's going to cook us a big dinner, I have an appetite for an old time meal like I used to fix. You've never seen your Momma make a big meal, now have you?"

The mongrel dog was the fourth in a line of companions that dated back almost thirty years. Each one's death had resulted in a vow, not kept, to never have another. She had lived to mourn the deaths of all of the humans in her life, but it was the grief she had felt for a dead pet that almost did her in. When Brenda Hernandez died, she was unable to make herself get out of bed for several days. The tiny Chihuahua had been her favorite, and the two of them had made a daily ritual of walking through the business district. She taking leisurely strides, and the small dog moving its legs like a centipede, at an almost imperceptible rate in its effort to stay close on her heels. The small pink dog eventually wore her hips out wandering around town with her master, and never again would she take up the daily constitutional with any of the other pets that would follow.

The current pet was the most humanlike, she thought. When she spoke, the animal would look at her face, ears erect as if it were paying attention, giving the impression that when spoken to the words were understood.

"Would you like for Momma to cook us a big meal? After I finish taking my medicine, we'll rest up and then we're gonna make a big dinner for that girl."

She took medication to regulate her cholesterol. Some of the pills were for blood pressure, others to keep her blood thin, and more to regulate the rhythm of her heart. She questioned why a doctor would prescribe all of the medication to a person as old as she, but the answer was obvious when it came time for her to write the monthly check to the pharmacist. Her skin was as thin as tissue paper, the veins protruding prominently. Every little bump would result in a deep bruise. The slightest rake of the dog's paw became an open, bleeding wound. It was difficult for her to look at her hands. Once so pretty and cause for vanity, now long and crooked, multicolored knot of ligament.

She took each bottle from the top of the oven, and inspected the label before lining the bottles in a specific order on the counter next to the microwave. The blood pressure pills first, blood thinner, cholesterol, and last the pills for her arrhythmia. Where she once prepared the daily meal for people she loved, she now heated cans, and swallowed pills in solitude, except for her canine companion.

Everything remained the same, all of the appliances just as they had been. The utensils still in their storage place, only the people were no longer there.

There was a time when three different grocers in the little town made home deliveries. Each morning she would place a call and have the ingredients for the day's meal brought to the house. They didn't have a refrigerator back then, and, in the summer especially, the Texas heat would spoil food not consumed in short time. By mid-morning she would have the meal underway. In the heat of the summer she would cook with the doors and windows open, a screen for protection, where now there were bars and bolts.

"I use to would cook a big lunch-time meal every day. Now, you never knew your daddy, but he worked over at the machine shop, he and your uncle both worked in the yards. At 12 noon every day the siren would blow and I could expect them to be marching up that sidewalk in a few minutes, hungry for a big lunch. Every man in this neighborhood worked for the Katy and you would see them coming down the sidewalk every morning, noon and night just like a parade."

As she spoke she read the chart for her medication and took the appropriate pills from the bottles making a multicolored line across the counter top. The dog wandered into the small dining area adjacent to the kitchen and lay down nearby the door where they could still see each other.

"I get tired of taking these old pills, but that girl is the reason I do it." The dog lifted its ears as if her words foretold something important.

She poured herself a glass of tap water and took each of the pills, finishing a ritual that was repeated three times daily. She washed out the glass returning it to the cabinet and then made her way to the living room. She sat down in the chair where she once read the daily paper. She stopped delivery of the local news years before. Old acquaintances no longer made the news. Instead, the familiar had been replaced by frightening accounts of crimes unimaginable to her in days long past. Once she became the imagined victim in every police bulletin, she decided to stop reading the *Herald Democrat*.

She sat in the chair for a few minutes to rest and the dog hopped into her lap.

"In a little while I'll get out some pictures for us to look at, but first I'm gonna call the bank and see what the temperature is." She picked up the portable phone from the table next to her chair and dialed the number of the automated time and temperature ..."time 8:47, temperature 42." The man's voice was familiar, and most days it was the only voice that she heard on the telephone. She called the number several times each day, and although it was incapable of listening or responding, it was a human voice to her.

She told the dog what the time and temperature were, as if it would somehow register in the canine's brain. She turned on the radio sitting on the table, and listened to the last of the farm report and weather...as of 8:30 the temperature in Wichita Falls is 28 degrees, with some reports of sleet and freezing rain.

"Baby, did you hear what the man on the radio said?...He says it's coming this way...I guess I should call over to the Basketeria and have them bring us some groceries before the weather gets too bad out there."

She dialed the number of the grocery store and placed an order to be delivered. On the other end, the girl told her that the store was extremely busy because of the weather forecast and that it would be a couple of hours before someone would be able to make a delivery to her house.

Having made contact with the outside world she got back to the business of waiting. Sitting in her chair she marked her time, the graduating increments of hours, days, weeks, years had been passed in that way. Waiting for the events marking the passage of time--illness, death, and distance were the benchmarks of her life as an adult.

The dim recollections of love, birth, companionship had long ago been overwhelmed by grief and loneliness. Melancholy, her most elevated mood. The determination to maintain a home for her and the dog was what kept her going.

After a short rest she got up from the chair and walked down the hall to the back bedroom. It was the room where the kids used to sleep. The furniture was that of newlyweds, sixty years removed. In the drawers of the chest were her photographs. She took two shoe boxes full of the pictures and returned to her chair.

"Baby, come here to your Momma. I've got some pictures for us to have a look at."

The dog came from under the dining table and positioned itself between her hip and the arm of the chair. The first picture out of the box was a sepia toned photograph of her and her little brother. Eighty years before, they stood in the dirt yard of a farmhouse somewhere outside of Sabinal.

In the background was a cotton field. The one where their parents had worked and the two of them had played. It was the place where her mother had shot a Mexican man who had been hiding in the mesquite bushes on the edge of the field while their dad was at the gin. In the picture both of them were wearing thick cotton leggings and looking scared into the camera. The fading image made them look dark complexioned, like Indian kids. As poor as they were, she wondered how her parents could justify paying money to the little Italian man who came by with the camera in his wagon.

The photographs transported her across distance and time to places and people familiar, and memories reawakened. In her chair she revisited friends and family, and could recall the smells and colors that the old photographs only suggested; their father with the rattlesnake hanging from the tines of the pitchfork resting on his shoulder, its tail dragging the ground, the picnic on the banks of the Red River where the reservoir now stood, the soldier in uniform, the baby girl being held by the young husband, the big ice storm with the cherry tree that once was in the front yard bent to the ground, the last Christmas when everyone was still around.

She lost herself in the images, and found it hard to believe that she could be the same person in the photographs. She decided to stop looking at the pictures when they became images in color. The color images were too bright, leaving little to be imagined, and less to be remembered fondly. They marked the cruel point in her life where strangers took the place of loved ones, unfamiliar people bringing bad news. Locomotives plowing into cars, and bodies found alongside of the road, and misdiagnosed illnesses, images of times more real than she wished to remember.

The passage of time went by unnoticed, hours like so many years. She placed the pictures back in the box, knowing that there was no one who could identify the people and places within, besides herself.

The doorbell buzzed as she sat the box on the floor beside of the chair, and the dog yelped the announcement of a rare visitor. She walked not to the door, but instead to the front bedroom. She peered between the blinds, identifying the person at the door before going to answer. A young man with the bags of groceries and smoke coming from his mouth and nose stood in the cold waiting for someone to answer the door.

It took her a minute to unlock the bolts on the front door. The young man entered the house, and followed her directions into the kitchen. He placed the bags on the counter and took her check before heading back out into the cold.

"Thank you for bringing these by."

"No problem."

"Do you have any idea what the temperature is?" she asked, as the young man made his way out onto the porch, pulling his coat collar up around his throat.

"The radio says that it has dropped twenty degrees since 6 a.m., down to 31degrees."

"You don't say...well, stay warm if you can." She closed the door on the cold and locked herself inside.

She took the groceries from the bags and arranged the contents on the kitchen table. As she searched for the utensils to cook the meal, she thought of the dead. Why she would be the only one to live so long was difficult for her to think about. She had tried very hard to avoid bitterness, and instead sought comfort in the knowing that they had been spared a great deal of heartache. She alone had lived to see things turn out the way they had. Never-ending waiting to see what would happen next. As it had turned out, there was only one more thing to anticipate and the pills prolonged the waiting.

The dog was skittish as her Momma clanged around in the little kitchen. She drug out the cast iron skillet and other long stored away objects as the dog paced around.

"Momma's going to fix that girl a roast and some gravy...after that girl has a good meal Momma's going to take her someplace special...would she like that?" The dog shook its head and snorted a muffled yelp in way of response.

The old gas stove warmed the room nicely, and flushed her cheeks under the thin layer of skin. The smell of the burners mingled with the aroma of the food gave the house an uncommonly festive atmosphere. The nostalgic smells gave her vigor. She chose not to take the afternoon medication. The busy kitchen was a welcomed change for her. A sense of control and the ability to alter the course of events gave her energy that the medication failed to.

The dog sensed that the normal order had been abandoned, and watched from underneath a chair as the meal was prepared. When finally they sat down to the meal, it was the first time in many years that the kitchen table had been used for its intended purpose. She gave the dog a plate of roast and biscuits sopped in the gravy.

"Oh we used to have such good times at this table....Your daddy would tell big stories and we would all laugh.....and we would play cards, or a board game..." She watched the dog eating from the plate.

"...when we finish with supper, we will go out in the yard and you can take care of business, and then Momma's going to take us for a ride. Does that sound like fun?" The dog had licked the plate until it shined.

The night before, when it was still warm, she lay in bed unable to sleep. From the Bois d'arc tree, next to the outbuilding out back of the house, she had heard the call of the screech owl. It was the same call that they had heard as her mother lay on her deathbed suffering with a belly full of tumor. Everyone in the family had heard it and knew what was meant. At some point, soon after the owl had called out, sleep overcame her and she awoke to the new day tentatively.

After they had finished the meal, the plates were washed and returned to their proper place, and the stove was cleared, the utensils put away. Instead of taking the evening medication, she rounded up the things she wanted to take with them. She found her coat and shoes and got them on before going to the back bedroom. From the drawer she took a shoe box of the photographs. She carried the articles with her to the front bedroom, where she slept with the dog. She selected a pillow from the bed and stuck it under her arm, and then picked up the flashlight that was always kept on the bedside table. She took the comforter from the foot of the bed, and turned off all of the lights on that side of the house.

"Come on girl...let's go..." the dog yelped from the kitchen where it waited for her to open the door as she did each time the dog had finished eating.

"Wait one minute...I've got to find the keys." She looked in the kitchen closet for the key ring that she had hung on the nail long ago. She took it from the nail and kept it in the hand that was free. She unlocked the series of latches on the back door, and opened it.

She undid the eye latches on the screen door and let the dog run out ahead, down the steps to the cold yard. She locked and closed the door to the kitchen and stepped down onto the cement landing.

It had started to sleet, sounding like falling shards of glass. The sky was low overhead, hard and indifferent. The security light shone down from a utility pole in the corner of the yard, illuminating the exterior of the building where the car was parked. She walked across the small back yard to the outbuilding, and once there tried three different keys before she found the one that unlocked the latch to the double doors.

She opened the door and put the lock in her coat pocket. The light on the wall inside of the building required her to feel around until she found it and, once located, illuminated a dim bulb hanging above the car.

"Baby...come on in here to Momma...come here now, girl." She set the blanket and pillow on the trunk of the car and went back to get the dog. From the door of the building she called the dog again, and the dog trotted up to the light spilling out of the doorway. She picked her up and walked back into the building, closing the doors behind them. The old car was covered in a film of pollen and dust. Dirt dauber nests had crumbled from the rafters, falling in orange clumps on the hood and roof of the car.

She carried the dog and placed it on the front seat of the car. She then sat the box of photographs on the seat next to the dog. She returned to the back of the car and turned on the flashlight before turning off the overhead bulb. For the first time she felt chilled in the cold air, the sound of the sleet on the roof and the wind hissing at the door, and the branches of the Bois d'arc tree slapping at the eves reminded her of how long it had been since she was out-of-doors in winter weather. She picked up the pillow and blanket and walked around the car to the passenger's side where she opened the door and dropped the items to the floorboard, locking and then closing the door. As she walked back around the automobile, she breathed deep the smell of the building. Old oil, vegetation, musty earth, people, a scent enhanced by time.

With the flashlight she located the ignition key and seated herself behind the wheel. She locked the door and pumped the accelerator one time. The car started on the first turn of the key and she let the engine idle for a moment before turning the heater on high. She reached across the seat and placed the box of photos on the floorboard. The cold air coming from the registers blew on her flushed cheeks, taking her breath away. She turned off the flashlight, and pulled out the lever that turned on the headlights of the car. The lights from the instrument panel gave the interior a warm glow. The dog looked up at her as if it expected her to speak, and she could see her own image reflected in the light of the black eyes. She held the dog's muzzle and kissed her head. She turned on the radio and moved the dial until she found a station that came in clearly.

As she slid across the seat to pick the pillow and blanket from the floor, a man's voice was finishing a commercial on the station - *why wait another day when you can act now!* The pillow was cold and felt damp in her hand, but she picked it up and propped it against the arm-rest on the passenger side door. She laid her head on the pillow and reclined as the announcer on the radio talked on. The dog came close to her side and nuzzled under her arm. She pulled the blanket up to cover them both, all except their faces so they could breathe easily.

The signal from the station began to fade in and out as it bounced off of the clouds from somewhere far away, but across the distance, she could make out the strains of an organ. It was the organ she had heard in the church. An old song, still familiar after many years unheard, made it to the car. As the static receded, the words came to her clearly...*ife is full of misery..dreams are like a memory...bringing back your love that used to be...tears so many I can't see...years don't mean a thing to me...time goes by and still I can't be free.* Like the box filled with the drab photographs the music was from another place in time. A place to where she willingly would be transported, if only she could.

The dog snorted and began to pant from underneath the blanket. For a brief instant she considered sitting up to turn the heater down, but she was comfortable lying there and a pleasant thought had just entered into her consciousness. It was only a minor detail, an inconvenience. The dog stopped panting and lay its head on her chest.

The Bois d'arc tree scratched at the building and the dog raised its head and looked at her face. She stroked the dog's muzzle and in a soothing voice whispered, "Baby, It'll be all right....just wait.…..... just wait…just wait."

Down to the Root

The road to Danny Ray Pack's house was littered with carrion. Greasy heaps of fur and bone lay where they had been struck by cars. Every curve revealed another mess, shiny black birds lighting to peck the oozing piles. Samantha Green had not noticed this before. She'd never ventured off the main road leading up the mountain until now.

If she was going to make a film about Danny Ray Pack, it would require establishing a relationship with *The Pink Man*-as he'd insisted on being referred to in their single telephone conversation.

"Yeah, if y'all want to come up here to take pictures of a freak, then you gotta call me Pink Man," he'd said.

"I'd prefer calling you Danny," she responded.

"Well I'd prefer not being a God damned Albino Nigger," he shouted, slamming down the phone.

The sharp words and the anger of his response surprised Samantha. She knew that this man was more than a character, and she couldn't make herself call again; she'd mailed a letter instead, informing him of her visit. Danny Ray Pack gave directions before getting pissed off, but she had no assurance he was expecting her, or that he'd be cordial.

Samantha was not an artist herself, but she'd learned from her family that artists like Danny Ray Pack needed people like her. By appreciating his work, and through her attempts to expose him to a wider audience, she felt connected to the creative process. Samantha was serious enough to establish a production company but had yet to decide what she would call it.

Though she had money of her own, Samantha believed investors would help legitimize her project. It had been easy to arrange financing. Friends of the family committed; now she was impatient to begin the interview process.

In their phone conversation, Danny Ray Pack seemed belligerent. It reinforced her doubts. This would be her initial attempt at art; and she was unsure of herself. She'd found inspiration and reassurance in the film work of Leni Rifenstahl. Samantha knew it was odd; that she, the daughter of a Jewish father, whose own father had made things easier by dropping letters from his last name, would bolster her confidence by admiring the style of a Nazi propagandist, but Samantha could separate the artist from the art.

Rifenstahl's cinematic vision, her sense of light, and depth were revelatory. While critics dismissed her work as the glorification of fascism and butchery, Samantha respected how the artist rendered the grotesque as beautiful. Refienstahl's later work, documenting vanishing African culture, captured Samantha's imagination. Her images of ash painted Warriors and the nubile women naked, shining like oiled onyx in the African heat, haunted Samantha. These were the abilities she aspired to as a filmmaker. She wished to see the truth behind Pack's art, and honor him as a worthy subject. This was the chance to focus all of her energy and establish her name.

Danny Ray Pack was an anomaly-he was pink, all but his hair and lashes, which were yellow as the paled hue of smudged pollen. He'd begun to emerge as an artist and personality. He was sought out. If he weren't pink, Danny Ray Pack would have been the lone black person living in Grayson County. Samantha found this vacuous existence incredible.

At first he made paintings, then masks, and now shadow boxes. The paint he applied to reclaimed plywood. He rendered simple figures, lacking depth, embellished with bold pigments available at the hardware store. His style became popular with privileged enthusiasts. Once he finished a piece, he looked for a place to leave it. He gave some to people he liked, the rest he suspended in the brush along the highway. People began taking notice.

Wealthy women, on their way up the mountain, stopped to take the eccentric artworks. They understood the appeal of the artist's crude effort, and within a couple of years Danny Ray Pack's art became valuable to collectors. The ladies started asking around, trying to locate the person who left those things hanging in the trees and bushes alongside the roads leading to their vacation homes.

Samantha's mother found the first mask Pink made. She noticed it sitting on a fence post just past the turn-off at the foot of the mountain. She brought it home and hung it on the wall of the mudroom. The face was fashioned of dried gourds. Tanned hide stretched tight making the fleshy, swollen purple eyes bulge, a gruesome tongue protruded from the mouth. It bore a striking resemblance to the tribal masks of New Guinea. The kind the young Rockefeller died trying to collect. Samantha's mother claimed to have known the young man before his disappearance. It seemed to Samantha that her mother attached a peculiar sentiment to the mask found by the side of the road. The face was hideous in a way that seemed appropriate hanging in the front room of the summerhouse.

Samantha first met Pink at a cocktail party. Her mother had invited him to bring his art to offer for sale. In the midst of the cultivated gathering of vacationers, he stood out like that which he was; an albino black man at a cocktail party full of wealthy white people. Wearing a second-hand Dashiki, jeans and brogans, he looked every bit the part of the outsider artist. The tanned women, dressed uniformly in bright floral print skirts, treated him more as a serious guest than an amusing curiosity. The husbands, sipping gin and tonics, milling about in madras shorts and golf shirts, avoided Pink, and ignored their wives fawning over his work. Before the evening was through, every piece sold.

Sprawled in an overstuffed chair, Pink feigned sobriety at Samantha's approach. She introduced herself, and Pink smiled, exposing tiny teeth, gapped like a toddler's. Even though he was drunk, he seemed to remember their meeting when she called him months later.

In this strange artist she'd seen the opportunity to distinguish herself. This film project could earn her the credibility she'd always yearned for. It would be her art, a definitive creation all her own.

Samantha pulled off the road at the foot of the mountain to check her directions. She knew she was close to the turn-off; she'd passed it many times on her way to her parents' vacation home. She opened the visor mirror, inspected her appearance, re-applied lipstick before letting the visor slap shut. Sitting in the parking lot of an abandoned store, her anxiety growing, she began talking to herself.

What if he isn't home? Will he remember me? What if he isn't very interesting? What am I getting myself into? Samantha took deep breaths, closed her eyes, thought of Leni Riefenstahl. Pink Pack was nothing to fear, not so imposing. As unfamiliar as he was to her, Samantha knew she wasn't going to find her subject to be un-knowable. This wasn't Africa. She wasn't readying herself to enter a Nuba village. She wasn't about to have her sense of modesty de-stroyed. She wouldn't be overcome by the odors of nude tribesmen, their exposed penises dangling in the dust as they squatted to watch wrestling matches.

I can do this. He is only some folk artist for Christ's sake. This is important. My timing is right. Notice details. Samantha gave herself a pep talk, and took a few more deep breaths before continuing on her way.

Danny Ray Pack's house sat back in the hollow, well off the paved road. As she turned in the driveway, the mailbox had "Pink" spelled in metallic letters, the same color as the name. Driving down the dirt road, she noticed several vehicles; old hot rods, jacked up with rotted tires, two old school buses, a dump truck abandoned on the side of the trail. Each painted with designs similar to aboriginal images--stick people, dots, dashes, and half circles that resembled the batik cloth she'd purchased in Bali. Words covered portions of the rusting automobiles. *Hunch that Thing,* all she could make out-spray painted on the side of one of the school buses.

The house appeared as she rounded a bend in the road. Before she got within twenty yards of the place, a pack of dogs descended on her. Big and little mongrels scurried and barked, until she came to a complete stop for fear of running them over.

She sat for a moment, not knowing what to do. Dressed in a smart suit, she knew better than to open the door, it was not apparel that would survive the pawing of a pack of dogs. Jumping against her door the larger dogs stood to see the driver. Slobber smeared the window, and long nails clicked the glass. The smaller dogs, the ones she couldn't see, were yapping and making the most noise. She could think of nothing to do except honk the horn and hope that Danny Ray Pack would appear and call them off. Just as she honked the horn, he appeared in the screen door of the small wood house.

Danny Ray Pack walked out onto the porch with a can of spray paint in one hand, and a can of beer in the other. Naked except for a pair of cut-off jeans, he glowed in the afternoon sun bathing the small porch. She marveled at the translucent pinkness of his skin.

He stood squinting; she knew immediately he wasn't expecting her. She considered backing down the driveway and forgetting the whole idea, but the project was too important. Samantha summoned her courage, she was willing to take risks, this was important.

The dogs lost interest in Samantha's car, disappearing when Pink gave a shrill whistle. Standing on the porch he never gave any indication of recognition until she opened the car door. He let loose another whistle, lower pitched--a catcall.

"Damn girl, where you been at?" he said by way of greeting. "I thought you done lost interest in me." He took a long swig from the beer before stepping down to the yard.

"No, Danny. I am quite interested in learning about your process, how you create such original works of art. Thank you for allowing this visit," she said. Wondering where the dogs were.

"Well, get your ass on in here and we'll talk about it all," he motioned towards the house.

The living room smelled of dogs, and had only a few pieces of functional furniture. Samantha took a seat on the Naugahyde couch. Rather than sit across the room, Pink sat next to her on the couch.

"You smell rich," he said.

Not sure how to respond, Samantha offered,

"How is that?"

"Your clothes smell like mothballs, but I bet your drawers don't." Samantha felt her throat blushing as Pink's buggery eyes grinned at her.

"You know," he continued, "You're going to have to make me some kind of a good offer to get your picture done. I ain't about to do it for free."

The pack of dogs scrambled up the front porch steps and burst in the room, nails clacking on linoleum. Immediately they made their way to Samantha and began sniffing her legs and feet. The big brindled mutt jammed its muzzle deep in Samantha's lap noisily smelling her crotch.

"Hey Big Dog, you smell them mothballs don't you boy?"

"I think they like you," he said as Samantha gently pushed the dog's head away from her groin.

"Danny, I'd like to get down to business here," Samantha said by way of defense.

"I'd like to get down to some business myself," Pink answered getting up from the couch, adjusting his crotch, and leaving the room for the kitchen. "Hey, I thought I told you to call me Pink Man," he shouted from the other room.

"That makes me uncomfortable." Samantha shouted back, abandoning her seat.

"Damn honey, this ain't about you being comfortable. It's about you asking to make a movie about my art. That ain't exactly grounds for you to be giving anybody ultimatums around here." The dogs followed Pink's voice to the other room, a small mutt lingering at Samantha's ankles. "The way I see it, you ain't no different than your momma and her crowd. It's pretty cute having some hillbilly junk hanging on your wall so friends can laugh at it. '*I could do that,*' I bet they say. Is that what you're up to? Wanting to make a movie people can laugh at?"

The comment stung; on some level he was right. The realization that this man was more intelligent than she'd expected embarrassed her.

The biggest dog reentered the living room and mounted the smaller one, riding it around the tiny room, grunting and hunching. Pink, watching from the door to the kitchen, took a swig from his beer.

"What do you make of that?" he said gesturing with the beer can. "Every damn one of them is a male. That's what happens when there's no bitches around. Big Dog shows 'em who's the boss."

She didn't know what to say. The smaller dog tried to free itself, growling and snapping over its shoulder, but the larger animal continued to hump the back of the lesser dog.

"Get him Big Dog," Pink growled.

"Can't you make them stop?" she finally pleaded.

"What's the matter? They giving you ideas?"

"No, it's just that it's making me uncomfortable."

"Goddamned girl, for somebody who invited them self, you sure do feel uncomfortable about it. Maybe you should just get the fuck on out of here and leave me the hell alone."

Pink whistled up the dogs, leading them from the room, a banging screen door sounding his exit out the back of the house. Alone for the first time, she took in her surroundings. The room was clean except for the reek of dog and kerosene. Other than the couch, there were two chairs covered in similar green Naugahyde. The only adornment on the walls, a large corkboard with miscellaneous things pinned to it: articles from the newspaper, a few rough sketches, invitations to Art galleries, maps of country roads. Red pins marked places Pink left his art.

Samantha brought out a small note pad and pen, and seated herself at the kitchen table. She looked over the questions she meant to ask Pink: Why the bulging eyes and protruding tongues on the masks? What is your inspiration? Where do you find your materials? She took a moment to collect her thoughts. She reminded herself to concentrate on details. Leni Riefenstahl didn't focus her camera on the most obvious things. Instead, she'd widened the perspective of her lens, allowing the viewer to choose what they wanted to examine more closely. *Paint on a broad canvas,* Samantha said to herself.

The kitchen table was bare except for a mound of oddly shaped roots. Samantha inspected the pile. Picking up a couple she was astonished how closely the root resembled a human figure. The limbs and torso were clearly evident as was a smaller appendage, which could be interpreted as an erection. The discolored root smelled of earth and a sweet richness. Ginseng had value. She intended to ask Pink where he'd gotten it, and jotted the question in her notebook.

Getting up from the chair, her attention seized upon a small box under the kitchen table. She recognized it as a shadow box. Inside, two root figures intertwined in sexual union, standing face to face. The bed of the shadow box was lined with green moss; a small creek fashioned of amber Mylar flowed in the background. The rear of the compartment was covered in what looked like a thin shiny mineral; she thought it might be sheets of mica. It was an eerie thing, at once complex and simple. The scene wasn't vulgar, as it might have sounded had someone described it to her. It was subtle, the manifestation of artistic sensitivity she so admired.

After a few minutes she left the house to find Pink, and make an effort to arrange another time when she could bring the camera and film him. She held out hope he would have calmed down, and that he would understand her interest to be sincere and not self-serving, but she'd already learned of his sharp awareness.

She walked around the house before sighting the barn. From the yard she heard the hiss of spray paint. The slats of the tired building were marked with varying hues of pigment; places Pink tried the paint before applying it to his work. Like the interior of the house, Pink's yard was neat except for piles of plywood and old metal farm implements stacked next to the barn-objects for his art.

She found her way to a door, tentatively opening it to the interior of the barn. Across the room Pink stood before a plywood board, his back to her. A fog of paint fumes thickened the air between them. Samantha watched him apply a coat of gray paint with a roller. The smell of paint so strong she wondered if it affected the artist, it couldn't be good to inhale.

A naked bulb illuminated Pink at work. She couldn't make much of the dark expanse of the barn. The best she could tell, the shadows hid boxes, planks of wood and plastic barrels. On the wall next to where Pink worked hung several masks, all similar to the one her mother found. The bulging eyes seemed to look past her from across the room. Suddenly light-headed, Samantha believed the paint fumes might make her sick.

"Pink?"

Turning slowly, he faced her direction with a smile. Teeth big and white, the kind dentures make.

"Now that's more like it," he answered. "I guess I owe you an apology," he tossed a spent paint can into the shadows and motioned for her to come closer. "You ain't the first one to want to make a film about me," he said. "In fact, I just got back from New York City a couple of weeks ago. I sold a whole van load of this shit up there," he gestured to the paintings and masks.

"That's very good," Samantha smiled.

"Yeah well, I'd like to help you out, but I got a lot going on right now. It might be better to put all of this on hold, I ain't so sure it's a good idea for you to come around by yourself anyway, if you know what I mean."

Samantha wasn't sure if she understood or not.

"I'm sorry if I've offended you, Pink. It's just that I believe people will find you and your world fascinating. I'd really love to make the documentary,"

"The what?" he interrupted.

"The documentary film," she continued. "I'd like to go ahead with it if you ever decide it would be all right."

Pink looked at her for a long moment before speaking.

"Yeah, I'd like to make a movie with you sometime, but I doubt it'd be the kind you have in mind."

Pink turned from her, disappearing into a dark corner of the barn; she couldn't see him until a dim light illuminated the area where he stood.

"Come here, I've got something to give you," he said.

Hesitantly Samantha approached; reluctant to offend him further.

Atop a blue plastic barrel sat a shadow box, the interior illuminated by a small electric bulb. It appeared similar to the one she'd admired in the kitchen. The scene was different though. The electric bulb reflected off the back of the box. A shiny lamella formation created mountains, giving depth to the scene. In the forefront, several tiny plastic dogs stood, each painted to resemble a member of the pack inhabiting the property. In the space between the dogs and the mountains, two ginseng figures copulated, one bent on all fours, the other behind it. Although graphic, the image was strikingly unique and in a way, beautiful.

"Here, I want you to have this," Pink said as he unplugged the shadow box from an orange extension cord.

"Maybe it'll make you think of me sometimes."

"Well, thank you Danny."

"Hell, there you go again," he responded with slight irritation. "I'd better walk you out to the car," he said, moving a few of the finished paintings from where they'd been propped against the barrels. Picking up a pair of sunglasses from the table where he'd been working, he switched off the light, leaving only the sun coming in through the weathered slats and open door as their guide to the outside world.

The afternoon shone bright and muggy. Samantha followed Pink across the yard anticipating the pack of dogs. Approaching the house, she saw a pair of the mongrels lying under the porch. Sides heaving and tongues dangling in the cool dirt of the shade, too content to rise; they knew her already. Pink stopped short of her car, and gazing to the limited piece of sky above the hollow proclaimed,

"Looks like a storm blowing up."

Samantha looked to where he stood, his pale body luminous in the afternoon sun, and in that moment he was scintillating, unexpectedly attractive, beautiful like an alabaster fetish, or a figure carved from stalagmite. For a fleeting instant she thought she might linger.

"You know how to get back to the main road?" he asked.

"Yes, and thank you for the shadow box." She said.

"It ain't nothing but a shoe box. Tell your momma to come back here for a visit, and tell her to bring friends next time." He lifted his glasses and waved, then vanished around the corner of the house. Samantha looked up to the mountain and suddenly felt the trees closing in on the little hollow Pink made home. Samantha drove slowly down the driveway. Barely noticing the environment around her, so deep were her considerations. Before making it back to the paved road, she'd arrived at important decisions. She would be back soon, and bring a camera. A few rude comments would not dissuade her. She decided what to name her production company "Greenbaum Productions." She'd reclaim her family name. She knew her vision was keen, that there were important things to reveal about Pink Pack's life and work. Stimulated, excited about making art,

Samantha slowed to a stop. She had to think for a moment before remembering which way to turn on the paved road. From now on, she would pay closer attention to details. She must become intimate with her subject and his universe. Only then could her lens reflect the aesthetic qualities of the unique art Pink made. She admired his work, and left wanting to include him, to share with him her aspirations. To capture his existence on film.

Turning on to the black top road, she lowered the windows of the car, and heard dogs barking in the distance. The day was flooded with brilliant afternoon light, making everything more vividly clear to Samantha. She saw things in a new way.

The pavement of the country road shimmered in August heat. Samantha wished she had a camera. The road to Danny Ray Pack's house attracted snakes. The black top glimmered with their dried remnants, flattened and fried in the sun; the serpents glinted, shimmering like sheets of mica.

For the Love and Money

"Lee, let's get in the water," Helen said, standing up from the picnic blanket. Her flesh colored bra and panties concealed less than they accentuated, making Kylmer Lee Hayes crazy with love.

He looked at her, and felt the most affection he'd ever known.

"Alright girl," he answered.

They were celebrating Lee turning thirty-three, sitting on an old batted quilt under the hot shade of a Texas cottonwood tree. Making plans and drinking beer from sweating bottles, they were at a private place overlooking a still body of clear water; land her sick mother-in-law owned. Lee had met this woman, a widow about his age, and found the place he had always wanted. He knew it was his chance at happiness.

Lee adored everything about her, especially the way she used long fingers to peel damp labels off the slick glass. He watched her pasting the sticky, glued paper onto the open page of her leather bound journal. *Brewed from pure spring water, From the country of 11,000 springs*, the slogan read.

The river they looked down upon was one of those. Artesian spring-fed, it gushed up from the rock cap of the Edwards Aquifer. The water was different than what he knew. In North Carolina, creeks ran red with eroded run-off. Washed down from plow scarred tobacco fields. The red clay bled into the tributaries, making streams shallow and swift. But the water of the Blanco River slowed clear and deep. Looking down from the bank, he could see the white rock bottom of the pool. The surface rippling, bubbling up from the lime-stone foundation of the hill country.

Going to Texas had worked out better than he'd imagined. Things back home started closing in on him, the curves and hills became too familiar, his world limited. He decided he needed space, and to leave behind certain people, and put distance between himself and his history.

Texas was a big place, full of possibilities. In the two years since moving there, he'd traveled most of the state. He liked the ochre col-ored canyons of the panhandle, but felt lonesome there. The sky was big, and he felt small and alone. The harsh, sun baked scrub brush west of the Pecos River was more to his liking. The land fell away, and the perspective on distance gave him peace, the horizon was lim-itless. But it was the central part of the state he liked best.

Not as thick or lush as Blue Ridge mountains, the cedar and oak greened rises of the hill country felt familiar in a comforting way. He wanted to stay there, learn to call it home. He had decided he wanted to make a life with Helen, and stay in Texas forever.

Texas smelled good. Every town had a tavern and barbecue joint. Oak and pecan smoke infused the air. The summer weather was hot, but not humid. The winter just enough to note a change of season. The moon was big in the night sky, and he liked the people. Maybe it was the broadness of the horizon that made Texans more open. For whatever reason, it was different from home, where folks were more reserved, less accepting of strangers, protected by hills.

On the bank of the Blanco River, he felt perfect contentment. Not wise in the ways of love, Lee trusted instincts telling him to make the most of the opportunity. He and Helen had talked about starting a family, something she'd not been able to do with her husband. Lee knew if it didn't happen now, it might be too late. He wanted her to have children that looked like them. He didn't want to return to North Carolina, to his old way of life.

Helen, he liked saying her name, how it lingered on his tongue like her taste. She was long and lithe, her body evidence of an active life. He'd loved only one other, a girl who hurt him profoundly. But Helen was no girl. Her wise face drew him in. Her throat stretched taut with tendons, captivated him like no girl could. She was the love of his life. He considered things he'd never known before.

Helen altered the way Lee felt about the world. She was patient, not quick to love. Their relationship developed slowly, in measured time. More than a year passed before they became lovers. The careful progression assured his affection. Eventually, she told Lee that her husband had been her only lover, the one man she'd been with.

Lee didn't want to share much of his history with Helen. He'd done things he wasn't proud of; things for money. He'd dug up sacred objects, and desecrated caves for cash. He had gone along to collect drug debts, and run around with sad whores. He'd beaten and kicked a man, run-over another in a car. He'd thought of many bad things, but never murder.

Lee was glad to be rid of that life. He knew he could do better, and moved to change his circumstances. He didn't want Helen knowing what kind of man he'd been before coming to Texas. It was a new beginning and he would do anything to make it last.

He followed her to the Cypress trees at the river's edge where stacked rocks dammed the flow. A few hundred yards upstream, the river disappeared underground. No one would float past them. It was a secluded spot. He took off his jeans and shirt, slipped into the cold water, swam to a large rock protruding in the middle of the pool.

She joined him there. They lounged on the rock, slightly submerged, the hot sun drying their hair. He knew a kind of joy never imagined. He didn't want to leave her, or this place. Life seemed too good to be true.

"I'm going away for a few days," he said.

"Are you coming back?" Helen asked.

"Yes, I am." He wanted to say more, but was relieved she didn't ask questions.

The night before, he'd called his father in North Carolina. His dad was sick, and had no one else.

"Kylmer, when you coming home?" his father asked, using his son's given name.

"I don't know, Pop. I'm not planning on it anytime soon."

"Well, you ought to know about Grady, he got in over his head. He's fixing to testify against a bunch of Mexican big shots. He ain't around, got put in the witness protection program." The old man coughed, muffled the receiver.

"Pop, what's that have to do with me coming home?"

"I'm sick, son."

"I know that."

"Before he took off, Grady buried a shit load of money. He asked me to bring my backhoe, dig the holes for him. This is your chance to get it."

He thought about what his father said. How he didn't want to go back there. "How much money you talking about dad?"

"I dug three holes, put a fifty-gallon barrel of bills in each one. I don't know for sure, but it's a hell of a lot. Enough to set you up for good."

Lee said he had a job to finish, told his father it would be at least a week before he could get there.

"I ought to make it that long," his father coughed.

Grady was Lee's childhood companion, and the brother of the only girl Lee ever loved. Their fathers were best friends, ran illegal liquor together. Grady had picked-up where his father left off, trafficking drugs instead of corn liquor.

Grady got in way too deep. Lee was almost caught-up in the mess before he left. Grady had asked Lee to fly to New Orleans, pick up a car and drive it back to North Carolina. The trunk packed with over a hundred pounds of cocaine, worth more than Lee's life. Having taken the risk, Lee felt obligated to accompany Grady to collect the money that was owed, but he preferred avoiding violence.

The man in Charlotte didn't want to pay. It was early on a Sunday, a time Grady picked for the element of surprise. The man opened the door wearing a bathrobe, holding a gun. Grady and Lee beat him down in the doorway, stomped and kicked him back inside the apartment. They took his gun, busted his stereo, kicked-in his television, and left him lying in a bloody naked heap. Grady got his money, but remained angry.

"I'm not good at this shit," Lee told him driving down deserted streets.

"The hell you're not," Grady said. "You don't give yourself enough credit, bro. You're real good at this shit."

Lee stopped at a red light.

"I can't believe that son of a bitch pulled a fucking gun," Grady screamed, adrenaline pumping.

A black guy stepped in front of their car just as the light changed.

"Look at this mother-fucker," Grady said. "Honk the god damned horn," he leaned across, did it himself.

At the sound, the black guy stopped, turned towards them, pounded his chest, said something. Lee revved the engine, hoping the black guy would move on. Instead, he banged the hood with his fist, lifting his shirt to expose the grip of a gun stuck in the waist of his baggy jeans.

Lee stomped the gas pedal. For a split second, the black guy rolled up the windshield, then the car accelerated, and he lifted into the air, tumbling to the asphalt.

"God damn, I can't believe you did that," Grady laughed, turning to look. "You knocked his fucking shoes off his feet," he said admiringly.

In the rear view mirror, Lee saw the still figure sprawled in the street, shoes flung wide from the body. Lee realized a part of his self he hated, and wanted to separate from. It was then, in that moment he decided to move away.

He ended up in San Marcos, a town with good bars and friendly people. He started a legitimate business, installing game-proof fences. Texas gave a tax break to landowners for running livestock on their property. Business was booming. New money kept him busy surrounding ranches with twelve-foot fences. He purchased equipment, hired Mexican day laborers, and began pounding fence posts into the rock hard earth. He earned an honest living, tried to forget his past.

He met Helen when she contacted him for an estimate. Living on twelve hundred acres, with river frontage, an exceptional piece of property. Lee admired her grace immediately. Even wearing a straw hat, the fine structure of her cheeks and nose were evident, her lips full. She tucked her hair under the rim of the hat, but a few sun-licked wisps curled down the back of her long neck. He saw she didn't wear jewelry on her slender fingers.

They drove the perimeter of the ranch, Lee noting deer lazing in the shade of live oak, and stands of cedar, places where rock bed would make the job harder. Her air-conditioned Suburban made things comfortable. They stopped to inspect the sagging fence. Lee followed Helen, admiring her jeans, the brass rivets drawing attention to where the snug fit her fine physique.

Helen stooped to pick-up something, and Lee almost stumbled into her, so surprised at the interruption of his thoughts.

"Look at this," she said, turning to Lee, handing him a flint blade.

He palmed the point, a very nice one. "Do you see a lot around here?" he asked.

"Hardly a day goes by I don't find a few." She wiped soil on the front of her jeans. "Mounds are all over the place. One's right there," she pointed.

Lee could see a spot in the trees where the ground humped.

"Do you mind?" he gestured towards the mound.

They walked a short distance, Helen stopping yet again to pick up an arrowhead.

"Are you interested in Indian stuff?" she asked.

He nodded, "What about you?"

"Ever since I was a kid," she responded, nudging the earth with the tip of her boot, "Look there," another fine point turned over in the dirt.

You didn't even have to dig, he thought. He was more curious than he wanted to show.

"Somebody dug-up one on the other side of the ranch. I hope the fence will keep out trespassers." She looked at Lee, almost smiled, but her gray eyes weren't happy, just her lips curling at the edge.

That's how it began. A shared interest during a chance encounter. He couldn't stop thinking about her. When she accepted his estimate, he began work with an anticipation never known before. He couldn't wait to see her again.

The job took three weeks, enough time to learn something about Helen's life. The ranch belonged to her frail mother-in-law, whose will stipulated it would go to Helen and her husband--now five years dead. Helen served as executor of the estate and lived in a handsome rock house on the property. She kept an eye on things, and helped her mother-in-law with her affairs. The old woman was sick and rarely came to the ranch. She had a niece that helped her too, but it wouldn't be long before the old woman moved into an assisted living facility. The ranch would be Helen's one day, if the niece didn't find a way to have the will altered.

Lee listened, remembering every detail Helen shared. When he finished the fence he asked if they might see each other again.

"Maybe so," she replied.

"I'd like to poke around the mounds," he responded, not wanting to leave things ambivalent between them.

"That sounds like it could be fun," she said. "Why don't you give me a call some time?" Helen offered her hand, and as Lee took it, she fixed him with her gaze. For an extended moment she looked right at him, her face expressionless, taking an accounting of him. Then she smiled in a warm, reassuring way, her blue eyes surveying his face.

For a week, he struggled to keep from contacting Helen, then she called him.

"Lee, I found something you might like to see," she said. "Why don't you come out to the ranch tomorrow?"

When he next saw Helen, she wore khaki shorts, an old denim work shirt, the sleeves rolled up. Her hair fell free, trimmed to chin length, she looked happy.

Helen told him what she'd found.

"I was walking along the creek, and noticed where the bank washed out during spring flooding. Bones are sticking out of the ground."

They drove to the other side of the ranch, and he followed her to a spot back in the trees away from the river. He liked how her shorts didn't expose too much. Her lean legs disappearing under the cuff of fabric thrilled Lee. Helen's strong hamstring curving to a taut rear convinced Lee he would follow her anywhere.

They stopped at a site where Indians killed buffalo. The erosion exposed skeletons long buried. Lee inspected the dense, osteal remains, most bearing marks from blades of ancient butchers. As he inspected the bones, Helen found a beautiful object.

Amidst the disturbed soil and roots of a fallen pecan tree, she found a large blade. Perfectly shaped, thin as a coin, larger than his hand, something magnificent. It was as if the craftsman were showing off, making it as much for art as to produce a useful tool. They found more wonderful things, enough to fill a bucket.

It was the happiest afternoon of his life. Discovering history and not trespassing in the process, sharing the thrill with a woman. He'd fallen in love with Helen, and her place. The afternoon with Helen proved they shared a hobby, and also reminded him of his past.

Two weeks before his birthday, Lee agreed to help a friend cut pictures from a cave wall. Brock knew of something special. It was a return to old ways he'd tried to forget, but he saw an opportunity to make money.

Brock was a former archaeology student, and he told Lee the university was documenting Pecos cave art in West Texas. Ranchers were encouraged to protect the sites but Brock knew of cave paintings west of the Pecos yet to be documented.

"Like nothing you've ever seen," he told Lee. "They look like amoebas, or paramecium, some kind of psychedelic hallucination," he said. Brock knew a guy building a mansion on Lake Travis. He'd pay a ridiculous amount to get the paintings so they could be installed above his fireplace mantle.

Lee accepted an offer to go see them. It was a five-hour drive, much of the time spent talking artifacts. Lee didn't tell about the finds he'd taken. He was observing Brock, sizing him up. A good judge of character, Lee decided Brock was all right, and might be a partner in a big score if the paintings were as odd as he described.

The caves were remote, in a God forsaken land as desolate as anything Lee had ever seen. Few plants lived in the rocky terrain, no animals. Brock drove along a washed out ravine, miles from the nearest ranch road. They hiked another couple of miles to the site.

The caves weren't like what Lee had been to in Utah and New Mexico, those high on cliffs. These were more like holes in the rock walls of the arroyo. Not cavernous, just opening up enough for a person to stand. They turned flashlights to the walls, the art every bit as peculiar as Brock had described.

The images were fairly large. Some bigger than a coffee table book. The colors swirled bright red, green, purple, and were dotted with lighter toned pigments, like nothing Lee had ever seen.

"Look at the shapes," Brock said, touching the odd forms. "Somebody was tripping when they did this, don't you think?"

Lee couldn't tell what the images were intended to be. They weren't human figures, or any recognizable animal. They were oblong, stretched, misshapen things. Most were fringed with hair-like marks, looking very much as something seen through a microscope.

He studied the contours of the rock. The surface was relatively smooth, flat enough to be cut. He figured that with a carbide-diamond blade, he could remove them in an afternoon. That became the plan.

Driving back to San Marcos, they agreed to return with two all-terrain vehicles, and haul in the equipment needed to cut the pictures from the cave wall. They both knew someone else would do it if they knew how.

Lee had agreed to return to the caves before having the conversation with his father. Matters were more complicated now that the time had come. He didn't want to go to West Texas, or drive back to North Carolina. Taking the cave art was risky enough, but digging up what Grady buried would be more dangerous. He'd look over his shoulder for a long time, but the money could make all the difference. Then there was Helen.

Lee didn't ask, but Helen volunteered details about her dead husband's mother. Facts that made Lee consider the future. The old woman's personality was changing. Her niece was now more her confidant. Twice, Helen was asked to contact the lawyer and alter the will. Helen voiced concern that the old woman might change it again, leave the ranch to the niece. Even if Helen owned the ranch, the inheritance tax would be so much that she might have to sell the property. Lee understood that Helen told him as a way of easing her worries, never intending to involve him. He'd taken it upon himself to consider how he could help.

Once, when the mother-in-law was out of town, Helen took him to where the old woman lived. The house sat in the sub-division sprawl of Austin, one more in a stretch of indistinct brick homes.

Helen checked up on things; brought in the mail, watered plants, read the rain gauge, recorded the measurement. Lee sat in a patio chair admiring Helen tending to the tasks.

Helen had reason to be apprehensive bringing him there. She'd said before that the mother-in-law would likely cut her from the will if she learned Helen had a boyfriend. He understood it to mean Helen loved him enough to risk it all.

Lee thought it odd that Helen didn't have a key to the house, but instead, used one hidden in the backyard. Maybe she'd forgotten hers, he thought. In the rock garden, below the rain gauge nailed to a post, Helen lifted a stone and took the key from underneath. Lee knew the hiding place.

He had a lot to consider. He wished he didn't have to go to West Texas, but that was something he had to do. It would be his final time taking artifacts for wealthy men's money, and it would provide him an alibi. He dreaded what would follow, the long drive to North Carolina; the awareness that it would be the last time with his father.

After telling Helen he'd be gone for a while, they spent the rest of the day in the spring fed river, she swimming laps, him thinking his way through what lay ahead. When he returned to Texas, it would be for good. He was finished with doing things for money. From now on it would be about love.

It was miserably hot removing the cave art, but it went fast. The power tools made quick work of cutting stone. In a single afternoon he removed four. The largest and most vivid painting, he decided to leave. A crack in the wall ran across the image, and Lee knew it would crumble if he attempted to cut it. In a small way, it allowed him to feel as if he had not ruined the site. Working in the cave, Lee never once considered being caught. Unlike every other time, ruining a site didn't cause anxiety. He was focused on even more serious concerns. As dust filled the rock shelter, Lee formulated a plan. His hands operated power tools, cut plates of rock from the cave, while his mind pondered how to get away with murder.

The mother-in-law was an old lady, but she might live long enough to take away Lee's future with Helen. He wanted a family with Helen, and to live on the ranch.

Elderly people pass away in their sleep all the time, just stop breathing. No one suspects a thing. A sick old woman found dead in bed, her house undisturbed. A daughter-in-law allowed to live her life, inheriting what she was due. A man securing a future before it could be stolen. Beautiful children born of love, enjoying the security of that place.

As he drove towards San Marcos, a huge moon rose in the east, craters so distinct it looked like a person could step across the void, walk the lunar surface.

They arrived at Brock's after midnight. Lee relieved to have the business finished. He had other things to take care of. He needed a shower, to change clothes and get back on the road. A longer drive waited.

Showering, he thought of Helen. Asleep at the ranch, in the handsome stone house where he'd never spent a night; their life together on hold, her loyalty making her wait, doing her duty still, for a dead husband. Lee wanted her to be safe. He planned to protect her, and make a comfortable life together. He soaped his body and shaved off every hair.

He put on a black shirt, a pair of dark jeans. He wore work boots with smooth rubber soles. He packed no other clothes. He'd buy more when he left his father. All he took was a pillow.

Locking the door of the trailer, Lee wondered if he'd spend another night there. Everything would be different when he returned.

He met no cars as he drove away from San Marcos. Only herds of deer crossed the beam of his headlights. The radio played a tune from his youth, a ZZ Top song he and Grady liked; *I'm bad, I'm nationwide*, they sang. He thought about his friend.

Maybe Grady was right, that Lee was good at doing evil things. All men are capable of killing, he told himself. Everyone can imagine a just cause; love was as good as any. He wondered if Grady had found love. He doubted it. Grady was a lot like his sister and love wasn't very important.

It was after three in the morning when he came to the old woman's neighborhood. The house was close. The lack of traffic gave him confidence. The world was asleep.

Lee drove past the entrance to the housing development, pulled in to a darkened service station, parked his truck among the others waiting to be repaired. He wasn't nervous. He tucked the pillow under his shirt, crossed the street. If anyone saw, he was just a bald fat man entering the trees behind the houses that all looked the same.

He wasn't going to be there long. Everything would work out. The key would be under the rock. He'd find the old woman sleeping, her head resting on a pillow. He wouldn't startle her. She'd never realize her smothering. In the end, she'd be saved the indignity of a rest home, the slow bleeding away of her wealth, and Helen losing the best years of her life.

He'd be a thousand miles away by the time anyone found her. There was all of Tennessee to cross. By the end of the day he would be in the mountains of North Carolina. Shadows rising like ghosts in the night. He would be with his father, who would die soon too. Together, they would take what wasn't theirs, money gained by Grady without the thought of love, and then he would return to Texas.

Lee looked to the full moon, the craters still clear. Texas was no closer he knew, but for some reason the moon seemed further away in the mountains of his abandoned home.

The moonlight brightened the back yards of the houses; he searched for the familiar patio, and he saw the rock garden, the rain gauge nailed to a post. The house was dark, no cars in the driveway.

At the patio edge he removed his boots. Walking to the rock garden, the day's remaining heat warmed his sock covered feet. He saw the place where the key lay hidden. He looked again to the moon, the source of illumination.

Raising one palm to hide the shadowed pits of the moon, Lee offered a prayer to the Gods of The Ancients. He acknowledged that by opening the old woman's door life would never be the same; and in the name of no prophet, he asked to be blessed. Lee pulled the pillow from beneath his shirt, and bent to the rocks, looking for the glint of metal, reaching for the key.

Reckoning Well

A full moon lit the Brushy, which rose from the property same as it always had. But from where Verlin Sikes stood at the back of the ruined house, the mountain looked different; it seemed to emit a phosphorous glow he'd never noticed before. The light made the Brushy appear bigger than its elevation warranted. He knew it wasn't much of a mountain--a hill really, but it appeared swollen and angry. It bulged, against the night sky, and he quit looking at it for fear it might erupt. He'd not been there in a while, not since the stone house exploded. He was there again to tend to unfinished family business.

In the week since he buried his mother, Verlin couldn't help feeling like an orphan child, alone in this world. But he was not alone.

The night was loud with the drone of cicadas, their call-and-response roared high from the tops of hardwood trees at the back of the property. The bugs' cadence seemed to make metallic flakes rise on Verlin's salty tongue. He tasted scabs-the tang of copper pennies. Grief confused his senses until time meant nothing and every day seemed a year. All week he'd mourned until he couldn't make sense of things. His head hurt and he was certain he smelled bruises somewhere deep inside, maybe on his soul.

The stone walls of his home place lay piled where they fell, only the chimney remained. The explosion didn't kill anyone, only a dream. His brother, Hub, had a plan. After their mother went to the rest home, he set up a lab inside the house making quaaludes and methamphetamine.

"Easy money." Hub'd said.

"Crank and 'ludes equal big profits. Truckers'll eat that shit up."

But it didn't work out.

Verlin's initial survey of the property showed the outbuildings still stood firm. He carried unlaced boots in his hand as he walked in the bright moonlight the short distance out to the barn. He stopped to admire the grapevine clinging to the boards, heavy with purple fruit. His mother'd made wine from the grapes, but it never had enough kick for her boyfriend Carl.

Carl came around soon after their father died. He was a different type man than what they knew. Carl was clean; his nails manicured and free of grease and soil. He wore eyeglasses and smelled of cologne instead of sweat, and dressed in clothes more suited for church than work. He'd been a barber they were told, but he never had a job that they knew of once he started coming around. They never saw Carl mistreat their mother, but he made it clear to the boys he had no intention of being a daddy.

"You little shits don't know how good you got it." He'd tell them when their mom wasn't around.

"What ya'll need is a good ass whipping." He'd say.

Verlin never understood the relationship his mother shared with Carl, but Hub seemed to.

"Mom needs him." Hub would say, but that meant nothing to Verlin.

Once when they were kids, he and Hub took a couple of bottles from the cellar. They carried their air rifles and took turns riding their pony, Dixie, up to the top of the Brushy, to a place where it leveled off and an abandoned apple orchard remained. They'd sat under a tree and drank the wine, watching the Shetland keep its nose to the ground eating fallen apples. First time they got drunk together.

The pony was old and potbellied, but it wasn't blind until Hub shot it with the B-B gun.

"Watch 'is" He said, drawing a bead on the pony's outstretched neck. Hub claimed he never meant to hit it where he did, a lucky shot he said. The pony jumped and bucked off a short distance, but didn't make much of it, and almost instantly returned to eating the apples. The brass pellet punctured the pony's eye leaving it looking like a rotted fruit, caved in and floating in its own mash.

When he learned what happened, Carl took a leather barber's strap and beat Verlin there in the yard next to the barn while Hub watched from his hiding place at the top of a magnolia tree. It was not the first time Verlin suffered retribution Hub earned.

Soon enough, the pony quit grazing and took to standing in the far corner of the pasture under the shade of a weeping willow. Protected by the canopy of leaves, it ate the foliage it could reach until the drooping branches were bare and more resembled roots. After a few days Carl moved it into the barn, into one of the stalls where it grew fat.

"Ya'll leave it be." Carl told them.

After months of standing in the stall, the pony's hooves began to curl grotesquely upwards, until it resembled a live rocking horse.

"Boys, this ain't right." Carl said as the three of them stood watching the pony. Gnats and flies swarmed the stall and lit on the animal's damaged eye, the pony shook its mane, but the bugs came right back.

"You gonna have to finish the job boy," he said to Verlin.

Carl led the pony out of the stall and into the yard. He tied the bridle to a limb of a walnut tree near the well and went back to the barn, returning with a rifle.

"Since you such a good shot, let's see if you can't hit that same eye again. Put the barrel right up there next to it, so it won't hurt as much."

He handed Verlin the gun.

Verlin took a deep breath, closed his eyes and pulled the trigger. Dixie fell in a heap, her legs buckling under dead weight. It happened so quickly that Verlin didn't have a chance to exhale the air he'd drawn until he lowered the gun and looked to where the pony lay, it's neck stretched toward the limb where Carl tied the bridle.

Carl removed his shirt and glasses. The boys watched as he took a chain saw and cut the pony into pieces, the legs first, then the head, making it small enough to fit into the abandoned well. The ground became sticky with blood as they stood watching the dismemberment of the animal, and Carl didn't look so clean anymore.

"You're a mean bastard." Hub finally said

"What was that?" Splattered by blood, Carl turned to face the boys, one of the animal's legs in hand, a long curved hoof pointing in their direction.

"You didn't have to do it." Hub said.

"Boy, you must want to get your ass beat just like your damn brother." For once, Carl didn't focus his anger on Verlin, or notice he still held the gun.

"No Carl, you ain't ever gonna do that again." Hub said.

"Shoot him Verlin. Go on now, shoot him."

Pulling the trigger the second time was easier Verlin'd thought.

They'd covered the well best they could. Good enough that it held up for years. Their mother never knew the truth about Carl or the pony and, if she had any suspicions, she kept them to herself. She never had another boyfriend either.

Verlin walked on in the shimmering night air, passed the barn until he felt grass covered walnuts under his feet. He knew then that he'd found the place with the hole in the ground, the old well.

"Hey," he hollered down, "is anybody home?"

"Got some company for you Carl, you old piece of shit" he said, and chuckled to himself.

The chicken wire and boards that clogged the chasm from when they were kids was all broken down now. He set the boots aside and easily lifted what remained of the covering. The time had come to fill it all in. They'd have to if they sold the place.

He'd hoped his mother's passing would bring relief. He wanted to enjoy knowing she was freed from the humiliation of the rest home, but that hadn't happened yet. He was glad to not go back there. He never again wanted to smell such a place; powder on old slippery skin and boiled chicken not quiet masking the stench of eroding lives.

Hub wanted Verlin to work. Said things needed taking care of, but Verlin was resentful. Hub hadn't attended their mother's funeral. What could have been more important? From her deathbed their mother called his name first.

"Hub, you boys be careful now." She cajoled the eldest, her favorite child, her pride and joy she called him.

"Ya'll don't go near that old well, and look out for them wasper nests" she warned. And to Verlin, the youngest, the one who was with her at the end, she asked this:

"You fed that pony today, Verlin?"

"Pinky, we're fixing to beat the shit out of you," Verlin said. Pinky bolted upright in a green Naugahyde chair. His eyes blinked rapidly, like they were controlled by an electric current.

Danny Ray Pack was Pinky's given name, but no one ever called him that. His skin was almost transparent, like that of a baby possum or squirrel, some animal that lost its fur, or hadn't yet haired over. A camouflage cap concealed hair as blonde and fine as that of a toddler. His weak eyes were shaded from light by the bill pulled over his brow. That forced him to tilt his head back to look at the man standing over him. Squinting and blinking, he considered Verlin's statement.

"Why're you going to do that?" he finally asked.

"You know better than to fuck around with Hub," Verlin answered, laying a meaty palm on Pinky's shoulder.

"I haven't been fucking around with him."

"Well, that's not what he thinks." Verlin patted Pinky and nodded to the kid who'd come with him,

"You need to pay up, cause if you don't we're going to have to put a hurting on you, that's all there is to it."

Pinky looked across the room to the kid sprawled on the couch.

"Where's he from?" Pinky asked.

"Where're you from, kid?" Verlin asked, although he knew well enough.

"Damn!… It's hot all up in this mug." The kid said as he stood, looking around the cluttered room, breathing air that stunk of dogs and kerosene.

"Don't matter where I'm from." The kid's pants were falling off his hips, making his long skinny legs appear dwarfish as the fabric bunched around his ankles. He took a couple steps, but stopped short of where Verlin stood next to the seated albino man.

"Yo, let's get on with it, so we can get the fuck out of here." He tugged up his sagging dungarees.

"What's up with this pink motherfucker anyway? Don't he know what time it is?"

Everything about the kid irritated Verlin. He talked like a black, wore sagging pants and too big jacket, and now here stepping into family business. The kid was foreign to Verlin, half the time he didn't understand what he was saying. In the car on the way to Pinky's, the kid never showed he understood Verlin and Hub were brothers. It pissed Verlin off that this kid thought he was on equal ground. But who's fault was that-Hub cause he didn't point it out, or the kid for being an outsider?

He was but one of a number of young folks, male and female, Hub had recently taken up with. They'd come up to Grayson County from Charlotte. Hub sent the girls out, sometimes the boys.

"Brother-man, I'm doing the homeboys a favor." Hub would say when Verlin questioned the plan.

"Hell-you know better'n me-it ain't easy to get laid around here."

But Verlin never liked it. Of all the endeavors his brother involved him in, however criminal, not once had Verlin questioned Hub's methods, until now. Moving drugs or collecting money for them-that was one thing, but dealing in flesh-that was common-Not something their people had ever done, or ever would condone.

"I don't want to know all of that fucked-up shit." Verlin stopped Hub from telling the details of Pinky and the whore.

"Just say what's owed."

Verlin was used to working alone and didn't want to take the kid with him.

"Come on Hub, he's a punk."

But Hub was dressing for the evening and didn't care about Verlin's concern. He checked himself in the mirror, smiling to make sure his teeth were clean, and turned to his younger brother, still smiling.

"Take him with you." He said, slicking his hair back and buttoning a starched white dress shirt.

"Help me out here, brother man. You'll be doing me a big favor."

Verlin knew the kid had a girlfriend that Hub was keen on.

"Goddamn, Verlin, she's hot!" he remembered Hub saying when he saw her the first time.

The girl claimed she hadn't been paid for services rendered to Pinky, and Hub wanted him to collect the money. Verlin knew his brother usually got what he wanted, and it was his job to help him to those ends. Verlin didn't mind pressuring people for money they owed Hub, but this was different. This was collecting debts for strangers, and he couldn't justify that.

"When did Hub start hanging around punks like this?" Pinky asked.

Verlin almost laughed. It was funny that Pinky would voice the same observation he'd thought himself. But he didn't laugh. The kid was dangerous.

"What's that bitch?" the kid took a couple of steps forward, his untied boots thundering like a draught horse across the linoleum floor.

"Keep grinning at me like that freak, and I'm gonna bust your Goddamned grille." He smiled at Pinky.

"Hold on there, Killer." Verlin, extended a thick arm, but didn't look at the kid. What Verlin hated most, was this boy's lack of knowing, of how close he might be to harm--maybe he envied him that, he wasn't sure.

Things weren't going like Verlin'd imagined. He'd figured by leaning on Pinky just a little, he'd cough up the money and that would be the end of it. But once Pinky started asking questions, Verlin felt energy leaving him. Pinky seemed to be inhaling it. Verlin could see it happening--a colorless vapor boiled from his chest and curled white, misty into Pinky's nostrils.

The kid was right. Pinky did look like he was grinning, his weak eyes drawn into a squint and his dry lips curled back to expose teeth, gapped and baby-like, favoring mealy kernels of corn.

Verlin knew he had to get control. Waving ham-like palms, hoping to clear this fog smoldering between them, he bent over close to Pinky's face. The albino, no longer smiling, stared back at Verlin with milky gray eyes, red rimmed with coarse pale lashes, which reminded Verlin of that Shetland pony. An unsettling feeling came over him. "I'm gonna feel real bad about busting you up, Pink," Verlin said, pulling up a chair and sitting directly in front of him.

"So take my advice and give us something to take back to Hub."

"I swear to God, Verlin," Pinky said.

"I don't know what you're talking about. I ain't got nothing that belongs to Hub."

"You're a damn lie!" the kid said.

"You never gave my girl shit you cocksucker. You told her it was free cause Hub owed you!"

When Verlin looked, the kid was surrounded by a sulfuric gleam. Verlin tried to dismiss the yellow haze, but it didn't go away. He felt himself losing control. What were these sensations he was feeling? He wanted to get up from where he sat and take leave of the room, but it was too far gone for that.

"Pinky, does the kid look yellow to you?" he asked.

"Has the whole time," Pinky answered, as if expecting the question.

"I'm ready to get the fuck out of here," the kid said.

"That faggot Hub don't know who he's messing with." The kid said.

"I'm gonna beat his fucking ass." He said taking another step towards them, placing himself within reach.

He never knew he was in danger, and Verlin was on him before he could blink. How quickly it happens.

Verlin was surprised. The kid didn't resist. Probably used to other people breaking it up. That's what they did in Mecklenburg County: talk big, but hope someone stepped in. At first, Verlin grabbed the front of the kid's jacket. The kid looked at him briefly, then closed his eyes and tilted his head back towards his left shoulder. Verlin took hold of the boy's neck with strong hands. Yellow haze engulfed them both. Pinky sat separate from the fog, watching what happened.

Time halted. Verlin felt as if he'd left his body. His hair sensed the rot of apples in the orchard on top of the mountain, he smelled Hub playing under the grapevine, and heard him wearing the Beekeeper's bonnet. He tasted his mother being bucked across the pasture on the back of a blinded rocking horse.

The kid didn't open his eyes until the end. His lips parted as Verlin hunched his shoulders, leaning forward, pressing the scrawny neck. Verlin felt the windpipe crushing under his thumbs. When they were kids him and Hub would mash the red mud dirt dauber tubes built in the barn, the larvae inside squashed white and green, killing both parent and offspring. Easy - no reason for remorse.

"Damn Verlin! You done killed him! Killed him right here in my living room," Pinky said. But Verlin didn't let go. He looked to where the kid's clenched hands reached for his wrists, and increased the pressure. The Kid never blinked again. His eyes bulged as they stared past Verlin. The ruptured veins turning the white of the eye the color of peeled grapes-not purple but almost. His swollen tongue protruded and a bubble appeared in the gap of his bluing lips. Thick and brown, it grew the harder Verlin squeezed; grew to the size of an apple. Only then Verlin decided enough.

"I swear to God, Verlin. I ain't gonna tell a soul." For the first time, Pinky seemed frightened.

"You've known me forever, and I ain't once ratted anybody out, you know that." But Verlin didn't answer. He stood transfixed by the deflating bubble, and how the yellow fog followed it into the boy's un-breathing mouth to disappear into the cavity that was his body.

Verlin took to his task with a lightened heart. The night was cool, the air ripe with sweet scent of grapes come into season. He picked up one boot, then the other and dropped them into the cool breeze of the well. He listened for them to hit bottom, but the yawning hole returned only a muffled reverberation, too faint to gauge the depth. He fetched the kid's body and dropped it in feet first. Echoes glanced off the narrow sides of the shaft as Verlin added stones from the pile of rubble, enclosing the tomb.

The night passed as he made innumerable trips between the wreck of a house and the hole in the ground. In the pre-dawn light the Brushy no longer seemed as large. He couldn't see it filling, but from the sound of falling rocks, the hole wasn't nearly as deep as when he started. He decided the job would be done when all of the stones were gone, even if the hole were only half full.

Matters of Honor

Somewhere, Mark Frierson is eating Krispy Kreme doughnuts, his fat face flush. Tiny flakes of sugar glaze glint in his wispy mustache. He licks full lips, and brushes bits of fallen dough from his shirt. I want to call his name, to demand he acknowledge my presence, but I always wait. I wait for the decision that never comes. My dream always ends before he gets the news, the word he is out.

Mark Frierson is a kid killer. I suspected it even before the crimes, and I never said a word. Acting on suspicion never seemed a good idea. Certainty, I have since learned, is the one false-truth to trust. Looking back, I am justified. But in the end, life isn't worth living if people get dragged-off because of another's unfounded accusations. And in my case, I'm prone to assume the worst.

It was easy back then for people to speak of him with contempt. Before the girls got killed everybody assumed him harmless, and by feeling sorry for Mark, they didn't appreciate his enormous unrealized potential.

Mark was a repulsive kid. His black eyes were surrounded by white flesh, like coal in snow, which in part accounted for his peculiar appearance - at once a premature man, a perpetual toddler. By the age of eleven, he stalked Main Street in his dead father's clothes. Decked-out in khaki dungarees, too big blazer and wingtips, he'd become a hulking slob even before the onset of puberty. With the change in his hormones he got even fatter, and his lip sprouted a downy brush of fuzz. The meat of his face swelled around dark eyes, until the flab threatened to cover his lids altogether.

In spite of having no endearing attributes, Mark was well groomed. He scrubbed twice a day, and his skin glowed like a fire opal. His full lips, redder than most boys, and wet, accentuated his lisp. Most people dismissed him as a big sissy, but he wasn't harmless, I heard he was mean to animals.

Back then, mom and dad owned Jackson Auto. They sold a little bit of everything, but not many tires. We were the first in town to offer appliances; refrigerators and stoves mostly, and reliable service. My father was a smart businessman, and the store provided us a nice life. A cabin on the mountain and a bungalow at the beach - my father made good after the war. He'd planned on my brother doing the same, coming home from Southeast Asia, and taking over, but it didn't happen that way.

Father was a crack shot, too. He proved that in the hills above Anzio, killing thirteen Germans in a single afternoon. They awarded him the Congressional Medal of Honor and a hero's parade when he returned to Elk Creek. He kept the award on display at the store, and people came in to ask about it for the rest of his life. Forever gracious when strangers inquired, he never said much about it around us, and it wasn't until near the end that he voiced regrets.

My brother Baine returned from Southeast Asia with a chip on his shoulder big as all of Indochina, and he dared you to budge it. It took him a couple of years to settle down. Running the store wasn't in the cards for Baine, and he came home only on rare occasion. He moved to Chapel Hill where he lived selling second-hand record albums on Franklin Street by day, and drinking beer and beating the shit out of fraternity boys in the bars at night.

I guess that was good for me. Having been born ten years later,

I never had a war, but instead was given a chance to make good on my brother's lost opportunity. I grew up working the register and accompanying the service guys on their calls. By eleven I could run the show. My dad even appreciated my idea to sell records and stereo equipment and let me choose the inventory. That's how I came to be around Mark.

He came in the store several days a week, flipping through the 45's, and admiring knives and guns in the display case. It didn't take much for me to play records on the stock equipment, and Mark's requests were undistinguished for the most part, except he favored English bands-Herman's Hermits, Chad and Jeremy. Those guys didn't get much airplay around Elk Creek, North Carolina, in 1970. Saturday mornings the old men came to the store. My dad kept a potbellied stove in back, and his buddies never failed to show up after getting their hair trimmed, wasting the rest of the morning telling stories and chewing tobacco while my father made busy doing odd chores in the stock room office. My father worked the key cutter the morning I first heard tell of what happened to Mark Frierson's father. The old men sat around a cold iron stove that May morning.

"I want you to look coming here," announced Chase Moore peering out the back window of the store. "The fruit don't fall far from the tree," Chase said to the group, none of whom bothered to get up to see what he was referring to.

I walked over to the window and there in the alley was Mark digging around in boxes behind Mrs. Eisenhower's shoe store. Mark wore adult clothes. By fourteen, Mark grew to the size of a full-grown man, and even though only three years older than I, he doubled my size.

"What you see out there, Chase?" Tamper Goins asked.

"It's that Frierson kid again. Look out below!" Chase yelled in mock terror.

The men laughed, but in a way telling me I didn't need to know exactly what it all meant.

"I wonder what possessed him to do it?" Tamper said. "I mean, a man'd have to be pretty desperate to jump off the Reynolds building, don't you think."

"Nah!" Chase exclaimed mockingly. "That poor bastard got so fat, Son of a Bitch weighed five hundred pounds. When he hit the street, thirty floors later, he popped like a tick. Wasn't nothing to scrape up. They covered him with two pieces of plywood so people wouldn't have to see the mess. Sat his shoes on top. When it got dark, they washed him away with a fire hose. All's they could bury was his teeth."

"Come on now Chase. Enough bullshit." My dad stopped him. "The kid don't need to hear that," he said nodding in my direction.

"Tom, just you stay clear of the likes of him," Chase said to me. We watched Mark take a fluorescent tube from the pile of boxes and smash it in the alley.

"See what I mean."

I'd heard stories at school - how Mark killed cats, tortured dogs. But on that day I watched him in the alley, somehow I knew our fates were connected. When two people share a secret, no matter how reluctantly, they're bound together, and Mark and I shared a secret, maybe more than one.

I hung around the store, taking over more of the chores, and at twelve I pretty much ran things. I threw a paper route, too. Each morning I delivered the *Elk Creek News* to people living near the business district. Most mornings it would be dark when I walked the streets - dogs, deliverymen, millworkers, the town desolate except for us.

One morning, I passed Mark sitting under the bridge across the street from the grocery store. Illuminated by a faint street light he motioned for me to cross the street.

"Get a doughnut," he said offering a cardboard box of Krispy Kremes.

"They're fresh," his speech impediment echoing in the hollow under the bridge.

The Krispy Kreme man delivered to the Cash and Carry each morning before five. A twenty-minute drive from Winston-Salem to Elk Creek, and the doughnuts were still warm upon arrival. The deliveryman left the boxes on the loading dock next to the store, and when the manager Mr. Jones opened at six-thirty, he'd bring them in.

"Yeah I'll take one," I answered before Mark pulled the box away.

"I'll trade for the news," he lisped.

We sat in the glow of the streetlight eating warm glazed dough-nuts, and they never tasted so good. I could only eat two, but the way the sweet dough dissolved on my tongue made me want to pack away the whole dozen.

"There's more over there," Mark said pointing across the street to the loading dock.

"No, I got to go, but thanks anyway."

Mark looked up and down the dark street before responding,

"Well, I guess I'll see you in the funny papers," and took off walking towards the creek.

Sometime later dad was making keys for Mr. Jones, when the grocery manager told him about trouble with people stealing doughnuts. Sweeping up in back, I overheard the conversation, but I never offered to tell what I knew. Even though I'd not stolen the box of doughnuts, I felt guilty I'd eaten two, and could have ratted on Mark, but I didn't. Now thinking back, had I told what I knew then, maybe things would have turned out differently.

With me taking on more of the responsibility around the store, my dad decided to move his office to the upstairs. From the open balcony his desk overlooked the showroom floor, the elevated vantage point allowed more privacy than the small space in back. No interior walls obstructed his view of downstairs. About the only time he'd come down would be if a customer had a question, or requested to look at a gun locked in the case. Most of time mom worked the register, but when I came in the afternoons and weekends, I handled the register and sold stereo equipment and records.

One September afternoon, the autumn rays of sun slanting through the windows of the storefront, my dad summoned us to the upstairs. He'd been feeling weak for some time, and visited Doctor Stuart twice in a week. That day is the most memorable of my life. That day I knew my father was dying and it was the day Mark Frierson came back into my life once and for all.

"I'm eat up with it," my father told us. Mom covered her face at the news, and my father, sitting behind his desk, let out a sob that resounded through the store.

"How long?" she asked, her hands still hiding her face.

"I'll be lucky to see spring," my father answered, and wiped his eyes with a handkerchief kept in his blazer vest pocket. He quickly regained composure; it would be the one and only time I'd see him cry. I remember looking down to the showroom floor and seeing Mark Frierson, lit by a dying sun in front of the gun counter, gazing up to where we faced our sad reality.

"Go see what he wants," my mother told me, and I left them to reconcile the news.

I probably wouldn't remember the customer I helped that day, except Mark's purchase came back to haunt the whole town. When the investigator questioned me months later, I told how he'd purchased a box of .22 caliber Remington shells, the same type found in the body of the girl.

"I need a box of bullets," Mark said, his slack tongue protruding through the gap of his teeth.

They found the first girl on the creek bank downstream from the bridge, just outside the city limits. In late September plenty of ground cover hid the place where her killer left the corpse. She'd been strangled, and then shot repeatedly with a .22 caliber gun. The paper didn't print the gruesome details, but I heard the killer shot the child in her mouth, eyes and private parts after death. A fisherman stumbled upon the scene three days after she went missing. Most people assumed a transient person; a hobo maybe, was responsible since there hadn't been a homicide in Elk Creek in anyone's memory.

The news captivated the community until the holidays; by then people became preoccupied with other concerns. Kids, who at first weren't allowed to walk home from school, began to visit the stores on Main Street in the afternoons, and people talked less about the murder as winter set in.

The shorter days made my father waste away. He'd been a tall, robust man, but the cancer took a mean toll. By Christmas, he looked emaciated, his eyes dull, like he saw things in the distance, but not too far off. Each morning he climbed the stairs to the office, and no matter how sick, he oversaw activities like a man putting things in order. He decided appliances were more of a future, and divested of all the tires, auto-parts, bicycles and kids' toys. The decision freed up space and he began ordering more appliances, stereo equipment, guns and ammunition.

Baine came home during the holidays, spending a couple of weeks with us. He'd wake early each morning, and sit smoking cigarettes and drinking coffee with our father at the kitchen table. The two of them understood things I'd never know - the glory and horrors of war. Baine, like our father, had been decorated for killing and given medals to prove it. But, unlike our father's experience, he didn't receive a hero's welcome, and found no reasons to settle down and run the store. He decided he didn't want a small town life. It all worked out for Baine, and during that holiday visit, he and my father made peace in a way I could not know.

Baine took an interest in my work at the store. Although he would never choose to work there himself, he wanted to expose me to new kinds of music.

"Hicks around here won't buy it, but you ought to listen to these records, Tom," he said handing me a box filled with second-hand albums.

"Which are your favorites?" I asked, pulling them from the box and studying the covers of the albums.

"It don't matter to me, all of them" he said, "especially the Dylan, and Flying Burrito Brothers."

It was the first time we made a connection to one another, one that would last until his death not so long ago. We found it easy to talk after that day, and it was music that bridged the years and distance defining our earlier lives.

We buried my father on a glorious Saturday morning in April, the hyacinth bushes still in bloom. In the two days since his passing I found relief in the finality of it all. On Monday, my father's obituary appeared on page one of the local newspaper. His death was noted in many papers, since he was one of few to have been awarded the Congressional Medal of Honor, but in Elk Creek it wasn't the biggest news of that day. They'd found a second dead girl.

They found her in a vacant lot North of town, where the bypass and Wal-Mart are today. The killer sodomized the child before crushing her to death. Tiny underwear still fashioned around her throat when the authorities arrived. It didn't take long to suspect Mark Frierson. The day my father's obituary ran, Mark showed up at the news office early in the morning, asking for a copy of the paper. A lady became suspicious when Mark stayed there reading the front page repeatedly, and she phoned in the tip.

My mom drove me to the courthouse to testify. Once seated, my eyes met Mark's, and when he winked, I wanted to punch him right in his fat lips. I told what I knew; about the purchase he'd made, what kind of bullets he'd asked for, and verified the date of sale. It came out in the trial that both victims ate doughnuts for a last meal. I never said a word about the morning we ate the stolen Krispy Kremes though, I never thought it mattered, until years later.

Frierson gave a jailhouse confession and it took the jury less than an hour to convict him, recommending the death penalty. Mark thought he lucked out when the Supreme Court struck down capital punishment; instead of a date in the gas chamber his sentence was commuted to life in prison. But nothing is ever final, nothing except death.

I haven't lived in Elk Creek for years now. I sold the store when mother died. Baine and I divided the estate. He lived out his life in the mountains; where the hills limit the horizon, and there he found his peace. I live at the beach near the lot my father purchased all those years ago, but I still read the hometown news. I scan the obituaries, recognizing fewer names as time goes by.

Recently, I read of a parole hearing for John Mark Frierson. Dumbfounded, I learned how few people in Elk Creek remember the murders, or that the confessed killer received a reprieve for his heinous crimes. Now I sleep restlessly; I'm visited in dreams; father, mother, and Baine talk to me. And then there is Frierson.

I used to envy my father and brother. Their shared experiences were beyond my knowing. To have fought and killed and been awarded seemed a distinction I'd been denied. But my dreams discourage me from wanting to make up for it.

"Don't even think about it," Baine tells me.

"It just ain't worth it, son," my dead father counsels.

And then there is Chase Moore, longer dead than any of them who says,

"Stay clear of the likes of him, Tom, 'cause you'll end up getting what he deserves."

Next week I'm taking a trip that will last two months. I'm going to Italy, where I'll rent a car and drive up the boot heel, crossing over to the Tyrrhenian Sea. Before I get any older I want to be in those places my father conquered. I want my chance to march up the hills beyond Anzio, and be where he found glory. I'm going to Southeast Asia, too. I'm taking a motorcycle tour through the places my brother wrote home from. I'll know the smell of rice paddies, the feel of warm rain and mud. I'm going to experience the foreign place Baine could not forget, and in the muck I'll look for pieces of what he left behind.

When I return there'll be other news to anticipate. The parole board will have made a decision on the future of Mark Frierson, and if he is given freedom, I'll take another trip, a venture to find him. I look forward to that meeting, maybe more than any other.

When I find him I'll not introduce myself at first; we'll just see how things go. Maybe I'll find the bar he frequents, and hang around until I learn the songs he likes on the jukebox. Once he feels comfortable with me around, I'll strike up a conversation, take his lead on what to discuss. I'll be careful to avoid mentioning his lisp, pastries, and cute little girls. I'll let him steer the conversation.

Then we'll get in my car, and listen to a few tunes. "The Weight," "I Shall be Released," and all of "The Guilded Palace of Sin." Whether he likes it or not, Mark Frierson will have plenty to ponder, I have serious matters to address.

Before it is all over, he'll know a thing or two. He'll learn nothing in this world is less important than the glory we seek for ourselves. We'll take a ride, and at the end, when we've arrived at our destination, I'll show him one last thing, and for Mark Frierson the horizon will look like it goes on forever.

Black Leather Jackets

Gus Ford missed running the beach-front beer joint. Now, he tended bar in a trendy place across the causeway from Carolina Beach, catering to the new breed of Harley-Davidson enthusiasts. He resented the clientele; their trendy leather outfits and gleaming polished bikes filling the parking lot, not a one of them would ever change an oil filter, lube a clutch cable, or get shot dead by a jealous lover while selecting songs at the jukebox.

Everything about the place felt phony. Even the name, *Iron Thunder*, seemed contrived. Gus loved the sounds and smell of a real bar; stale smoke, sour beer, the crack and crash of pool balls, and beer bottles, this place didn't have it. *Iron Thunder* smelled like newly varnished wood, and honey mustard chicken wings, the jukebox sat silent most of the time. Flat screen television panels showing car races and football games. Gus didn't know how much longer he could do it.

Gus carried the pitcher of beer to a table of young guys. He didn't really acknowledge them, just sat the tray on the table, and returned to the bar. He was going through the motions; he had a lot on his mind.

For several years, tending bar had kept Gus from drinking. He found there was nothing like dealing with drunks to help him forego alcohol. But he'd started back since the *Black Leather Jacket* closed. In over twenty years, he'd only worked one other job, turning spindles in a rocking chair factory. He drank like a fiend that year he was married; it was when he lost his scalp, and after that the Bikers began calling him Guster.

He often felt like he'd heard it all before and wanted to stop drunks from using him as their sounding board, a two-dollar-tip shrink. Barroom Psychology had become a burden. He learned to keep serving drinks, wiping down the drink sweat from the bar, and listening to what people had to say. His regular customers knew that taking off his bandana meant he couldn't stand it anymore. Recently, he'd started taking longer smoke breaks, stealing a drink of whiskey to help him through the shift, more in the evening when he got back to the closed-down bar with the couch in the back room.

A young man in a dust-covered Kevlar touring suit took a seat at the bar. Gus figured he rode in on a BMW, he looked the type and stood out in the crowd of lawyers, investment bankers, and their trophy wives all dressed in showroom leather gear.

"What can I get you?" Gus asked.

"A Bass Ale," the guy said

"Coming right up," Gus smiled as he turned to go to the cooler. Bass Ale wasn't on tap at the *Black Leather Jacket*, but it was just another fancy beer at *Iron Thunder*. Gus liked that this guy knew what he wanted. He had expensive taste, and wasn't ordering a Pabst Blue Ribbon in a bottle just to be slumming around, pretending to live the wild life. Gus liked that quality in people, being true.

He poured the pint glass, set it in front of the guy, and asked, "Want to start a tab?"

"No, I'll pay," he told Gus, pulling a twenty dollar bill from a zipped pocket on the sleeve of his jumpsuit. "I'm looking for a fellow by the name of Gus Ford. Is he working today?" the young man asked.

Gus turned his head and looked at the younger man sideways, making full effect of his arched eyebrows, a posture that put people on edge. "Who's asking?" he responded.

"He used to work with my father," the younger guy said. "He should be expecting me."

Gus noticed the resemblance: the square jaw, the curly dark hair, features of the father, his dead friend. The only difference, the eyes. The son had the bright blue irises of his mother, not the piercing black eyes of his father.

"My name is Roland Jones," he said. Gus stood nodding his head, pursing his lips, looking like he knew something, feeling like they'd both been there before.

"You found him," he said, sticking out his hand. "I'm Gus Ford. It's nice to meet you, Roland."

The young man drank beer, ate bowls of pretzels while Gus tended bar and maintained a running dialogue, telling Roland the difference between the *Black Leather Jacket* and *Iron Thunder*.

"A bunch of fucking dentists and lawyers," he said gesturing with his chin at the room of people, leaning back against the tap, pulling another pitcher of draft from the spout.

"These queers wouldn't last a minute at the Black Jacket," he said. "Your old man took no shit, Roland. His joint was the real deal. This is all play acting." he said. "We'll head over there, if you want. I'm about done with this bullshit." Gus wiped his hands on a bar towel and noticed the striking resemblance between Roland and Sully, his dead father.

Gus took Roland to the *Black Leather Jacket*, turned on the neon lights, and showed him the place. The large room was filled with meticulously catalogued motorcycle parts Sully had purchased from the families of dead patrons, or accepted as collateral for un-paid bar bills and back room loans.

Following instructions, Gus had emptied four storage units, twenty truckloads filled with frames, side cars, engines, mufflers, gas tanks, reflectors, every conceivable part that makes up a motorcycle. The grease slicked boxes housed one-of-a-kind machinery. Gus arranged everything according to a detailed schematic Sully drew-up. The entire collection now displayed in the middle of the bar according to make and model; rows of Norton, BSA, Harley-Davidson, and Indian pieces. In the back of the room, where pool tables had once been, leaned vintage bikes in varying degrees of restoration, lined-up in the shadowed vacant space.

Though he didn't ride, Sully found out his son loved motorcycles. This ironic twist of fate was a torturous part of his circumstance. Patrick Sullivan collected precious things for a son he never knew, and he offered cash to the families of dead or dying bikers. The poker runs raised donations that helped out the families. He gave them money for the order in life that might never be put together again and removed the evidence of the dead loved one from their homes.

That first night, Roland looked at what his father collected for him. He didn't have much to say, just walked the rows of parts and thumbed through stacks of shop manuals, catalogues, the boxes of gear. He slept on the worn-out couch in the back, while Gus stretched his aching frame out on the padded bench seat someone had bolted to the floor in the middle of the room.

Gus was happy to have Roland around. After a couple of days, they'd settled into a routine. Gus went to work each day, and Roland spent his time photographing various parts of the collection. Using a digital camera he transferred the images to his laptop computer. Posting the parts to an online auction was the final step and he sat back and drank six beers when the job was completed. By the end of the first week checks began arriving in the mail, and Roland began boxing parts and shipping the merchandise all over the world.

At first, Gus thought the virtual auction was strange. That Roland would sell-off a collection of a lifetime showed he was a businessman, cold, calculating following his rational nature. But what else could he do? It was his to do with as he wanted. Sully had left it to him, and Roland had nothing else coming his way. Gus looked forward to getting back to the *Black Leather Jacket* each afternoon to see what Roland had sold that day. It was fascinating to Gus, to learn about online commerce, and to find out the value of each piece of the two-wheeled ghost treasures.

"Look at all this stuff," Roland said to Gus. "People all over the world are looking for these parts. They don't make them anymore," he said.

Gus had no idea how such high tech global marketing worked. He watched Roland working meticulously with his computer and camera. What thoughts went through a young man's head who had been disinherited by the only father he had ever known, only to learn the identity of his real father? Rethinking one's paternity was more complicated than a barroom shrink could help the young man to consider.

Gus watched Roland take digital photographs of a '39 knuckle-head engine block, a stack of Triumph gas tanks, an ancient saddle seat off an old Indian.

"How much you think those will go for?" Gus asked.

Roland's camera flashed, and he said, "No telling. Yesterday, a guy in Japan bid $850 for this," and he handed Gus a corroded speedometer off a '47 Enfield. "Some idiot in Sweden paid 350 bucks for rubber foot pegs for a '55 Indian Apache."

Roland took a couple more photographs while Gus marveled at the notion that the boxes of forgotten parts would fetch that kind of money. The single speedometer was more than he made in two weeks at *Iron Thunder*.

"It's amazing," Roland said. "Look at all of this shit." He gestured to the room filled with old bikes, piles of mufflers and tire rims, stacks of boxes holding every imaginable assortment of cables, rod bearings, shop manuals, pistons, fenders and ray gun mufflers.

"You know, Gus, this is incredible. I would have never believed I had a father that ran a beer joint, and collected motorcycle parts. Un-fucking believable!" Roland looked at Gus for a long moment before asking his first question about Sully.

Roland tilted his head to the side and stared at the wood plank floor.

"Gus, do you have a picture of my father?" Roland asked. "I don't even know what he looked like."

"I'm not sure. There might be one around here somewhere. We

used to keep some pinned on the wall over there, but I don't know what became of those. Boy, if you want to know what he looked like, find a mirror. You're just like him, except your eyes. His were black."

Roland considered what Gus said, and then he asked another question. "Gus, did you ever see my parents together? In the same room?" he asked.

"Yes, I did. I met your mother at one of the gallery shows where your dad used to sell his paintings. Your mother had her paintings there, too."

"I didn't know that he was a painter," Roland said.

"That's how they met. Roland, certain people are magnetic, you can't help but look at them. Your parents had an aura. Some people try to draw attention to themselves, but they are just a loud noise. Other people make a silent roar. Your mom and dad were like that."

Roland put his camera down, and looked around the room.

"What did my dad paint? I mean, what kind of art?"

"Well, when I first met him he did these large canvasses, landscapes mostly. Then later on he stuck with portraits, you, your mother. They're all stored in the back room. He wanted your mother to know about them." Gus hadn't thought much about Sully's art. Painting was just what he did most of the time, especially after he stopped working the bar.

Roland was silent for a while. "My mother paints landscapes, beach scenes mostly," he said. "I guess it was the only connection they maintained."

"That, and you, Roland," Gus responded. "It must have been a hell of a secret to keep. What did her husband do when he found out?"

"I think he suspected something all along. We never got along too good, and I think he was relieved to know. He cut me loose, but he and mom are still together. It is a shame really."

"What do you mean?"

"I mean what a wasted life. My mom paints her pictures, and he doesn't give a damn. Never even looks at them. And all the while she loves someone else. It's a hell of a thing to find out." Roland shook his head and walked to the back room, to where his father's paintings were stored.

Gus left him alone for a while. He walked down the beach to the pier and bought a quart bottle of beer. He strolled to the end of the wooden structure and took a seat on a fish scale crusted bench. He sipped his beer and watched the old black ladies catching spots, take them off the hook and toss them into the five gallon plastic buckets of sea water they carried with them.

He took off his bandana and let the last of the warm November sun shine on his scarred scalp. He liked how the salty air felt on his tender flesh. He sat for a moment with his eyes closed and allowed himself to consider the possibility of re-opening the *Black Leather Jacket* with Roland as his new partner.

Until that moment, he'd never thought about it before, but out of nowhere, he thought how nice it would be having a son. He hoped Roland would decide to stay in Carolina Beach, and that resulted in the notion of opening up the bar again. He knew it wasn't likely to happen, but maybe so.

He gazed out at the darkening ocean swells, and looked back towards the land and the setting sun. He could see the last rays of day glinting off the metal roof of the building where Roland surveyed what had been left to him. He knew the beach-front lot was valuable. A developer would pay a fortune to tear down the building and erect a condo on the spot. He was happy for Roland that his father had left him something of value, replacing what had been denied by his mother's husband.

He walked back down the pier finishing his beer, and dropped the empty bottle into a rusting trash can swarming with flies. He could smell the rotting stench of bait left inside the galvanized can, and he wondered why someone would not just throw the fish out to sea; it seemed a thoughtless act, stinking up the place with fish that could be floating on the waves. He thought about this and how much people disappointed him.

As he walked back toward shore, he considered how little affection he'd felt for people, and he thought it a shame. The woman he married and Patrick Sullivan were the only two people in his adult life he'd cared for, and acknowledging that made him feel lonely. He was ready to get back to Roland. He enjoyed his company.

Roland was playing the jukebox, drinking a beer when Gus got back.

"You're standing in a dangerous place," Gus said.

"What do you mean?" Roland asked from where he stood looking at the selection of song choices on the old Wurlitzer.

"You're standing on the spot where the Dancing Bear got shot." Gus told him. "Look at that article pinned to the wall," he said. The yellowed newspaper clipping told of the shooting. Gus had placed the article on the wall right where the killing took place. Small holes in the wallboard surrounded the article, places where the buck shot sprayed through the Dancing Bear's leather jacket.

"Damn! This place was rough," Roland said after he finished reading. "He got murdered right here?" he asked.

"Ain't it a shame?" Gus said. "It's good to hear tunes playing in here again," he said. "Your dad picked all of them songs. He liked Merle Haggard a lot."

Roland turned towards Gus, and walked to where he was sitting at the bar. He sat down next to him, and leaned his back against the bar.

"Damn, Gus, I'm having a hard time figuring this all out," he said. "I've been looking at those paintings back there, and then you walk back in this room and it doesn't seem to fit?"

"I'm not sure I'm following you there, Roland," Gus got up to look for a bottle of whiskey hidden behind the bar. "But I guess you've got a lot you're trying to figure out these days," he said, and offered Roland the bottle of Rebel Yell. "This used to be my favorite," he said as Roland studied the label.

"I guess what I'm not able to figure out is just what kind of man my father was. I mean, those paintings don't look like something a man that owned a biker bar would be able to create. That's pretty fine art back there," Roland said raising his eyebrows towards the back room door.

"Your dad was a different kind of cat," Gus said. "He could kick a man's ass out the door, and then go paint a picture of you, and get to crying. He was just as comfortable listening to a country song in this place, or sipping wine at a snooty art gallery opening. I never met anyone like him."

Roland took a drink from the bottle of whiskey, handed it back,

"Gus, how'd you lose your hair?"

"Well, I quit working for your dad one time and I got myself married and took a job in a rocking chair factory turning spindles on a lathe. One morning I rolled in with a horrible hangover, and I got distracted. I dropped one of the spindles, and bent to pick it up, and when I did my ponytail got caught in the machine, and whoosh. It ripped the son of a bitch right off my head, slung the whole thing across the room."

"You still got the scalp?" Roland asked.

"Fucking A," Gus said, walking to the place behind the bar where the braided length of hair hung from a nail. He brought it to Roland, laid it on the bar.

"It yanked off so fast I didn't feel it at first," Gus said.

Roland picked up the scalp, felt the dried remnant of skin attached to the thick hair. The shriveled flesh, now just a scab looking like leather.

"Have you ever thought of selling it?" Roland asked.

"Who in the hell would want it?" Gus laughed.

Roland brought out his digital camera.

"Hold it in up there," he told Gus, focusing the camera on the blonde ponytail contrasting the black and orange backdrop of the Harley-Davidson flag draped on the wall behind the bar. Roland took a couple of pictures while Gus held the ponytail out from his body; his amputated scalp dangling like a dead copperhead.

Gus was smiling, a hint of surprise in his voice when he said, "Damn, I used to have hair," and turned to Roland with tears in his eyes.

"Is it alright if I put this on line, see what kind of bids people place? What would you take for it?"

"I've been dragging that thing around for years," Gus responded. "I'd take fifty bucks for it." He said.

Gus reclined on the old pickup truck bench seat in the middle of the room. He'd bolted it to the plank floor years before. It was the best seat in the house. Drunks that nodded-off there were routinely shoved to the floor for being sloppy in the midst of the lively setting. He stretched and surveyed the familiar room.

Gus felt comfortable on the bench seat, being back in the room where he'd spent so much of his life. He remembered the night Dancing Bear passed out on the same bench. How the bar was full of people dancing, and that it was the next to the last rest Dancing Bear would get, that he would be shot dead less than an hour later as he stood at the juke box.

Roland snapped a shot of an Indian Chief front fender he'd propped against a Norton Commando. The flash of the light illuminating for a moment the black leather jackets lined on the wall behind the bar.

"How long you going to stick around?" Gus asked.

"I don't know. This might take a while. There is so much here to sell," Roland looked around the bar, and all the stuff stacked in rows. "Gus, how did he come to have all of this?"

Gus crossed his feet, made himself more comfortable on the bench. "Well, he opened the bar after he got out of the Marine Corps. That would have been about '71. There wasn't nothing much here then, except the pier, a row of fishing shacks and a couple of the beach music clubs. I don't remember what he paid for the lot, but it wasn't much. He built this bar for twenty thousand dollars. This is probably a million dollar piece of property these days."

"I hadn't thought about that," Roland said. He took a seat on the old engine block. "I mean, how did he get all of these motorcycle parts? Did he ride? Did he build bikes?"

"Sully used to ride when we first met. But he gave it up. Most of the guys that hung around here worked on bikes. Some of them were always building a couple at a time. Sometimes guys needed money, and your dad would offer a fair price. Sometimes he took the stuff as collateral. A lot of it came from Dancing Bear's mom and dad. When he got killed, he left a huge collection at their house, where he still lived. Sully took it off their hands, and really helped them out. Most of what is here came from the Bear."

Gus was beginning to feel the whiskey; he liked getting drunk again. He'd done a good job for years, and now he didn't give a damn. He watched Roland behind the bar, and lay back against the arm rest of the bench seat. Roland had noticed the jackets hanging on the wall next to the Harley-Davidson flag.

"Gus, what's the story on these?" he asked from behind the bar. He was touching one of the jackets displayed on the wall. Twelve of them hung from a long coat rack bar bolted into the wall joists.

"Them are skins," Gus called out across the room. His voice echoing off the metal bike frames, the empty booths on the far wall hidden in shadows. "It's kind of a shrine to dead patrons." He said as Roland turned one of the jackets to look at the back. A flash from the camera illuminated the wall in a split second of blue light.

Gus got up from the bench and took his bottle of liquor to the bar. He sat on a stool watching Roland touching each one of the black leather riding jackets.

"It was a tradition your father started," he said.

"When Jimmy Groce got run-over, the only thing that didn't get busted was his jacket. It's the one over there," he pointed the bottle.

Roland walked to the end of the row of jackets, and took it down from the hanger. It was worn-in, some of the black having been replaced by a gray patina.

"Look in the chest pocket, Gus said.

He watch as Roland unzipped the pocket and took out a soiled envelope.

"Each one of them has a photograph, and a story of the guy that wore it, kind of like an obituary," Gus said. "The girlfriend, or wife, or brother, one time a father, they would bring the jackets in after the funeral. Your dad started displaying them, having a happy hour in their honor. We started calling it The Black Leather Jacket Wall of Fame. You wouldn't believe how many people would come just to check it out."

Roland looked at the photograph of Jimmy Groce the edges beginning to curl, and he silently read the short history of the dead biker before speaking. "Man, there is no telling what these would bring. It's kind of morbid, but there are a lot of people that are nostalgic for this kind of stuff."

"Dead American Biker Culture," Gus said, and laughed, and turned up the bottle. "People are phonies these days, Roland. They just want to pretend. This place holds the spirits of men that did it for real. There are ghosts in here," he said, and took another drink.

Roland was still looking at the motorcycle jackets, and opening another beer. The jukebox was playing an Allman Brother's song, and for the first time he could remember, Gus was feeling like everything was going to work out.

"Hey Roland," he called out his eyes closed. "We could open this joint back up, you know that?"

"It is a pretty damn cool bar," Roland said. "That could be an idea."

"We'd have to change the name though. It would be unlucky to keep it the same name," Gus said.

"What would you call it?" Roland asked, and took a couple of close-up photos of the jackets.

"How about this, *Guster's Last Stand*," Gus said.

Roland laughed at that, and came out from behind the bar.

He straddled an old Triumph sitting in the shadows of the back of the bar. Gus could barely make him out across the room. The jukebox had gone silent.

"Gus, there is a lot of motorcycle parts here to sell," Roland said. "Maybe you could help me out with packaging things up, and photographing the parts. I'll show you how to use the computer, too," he said.

Gus was feeling drunk, and had closed his eyes. He was recalling things from the past. "Let me think about it," he said.

He was thinking about the girl at the bar, the one with teardrop tattoos. She'd have been more at home in the Black Leather Jacket than the new place. So was Gus. He could hear Roland taking photographs, and metal parts clanging as Roland picked things up and moved them around, making money from what he'd been left.

Gus was remembering. Memories came to his mind like flashing still frames. Dancing Bear's size thirteen engineer boots turned out at an odd angle as he lay dying; Creedence blaring from the speaker,

"Fortunate Son"; Sully's glowing face that night in the art gallery; Roland's beautiful mother looking at Sully with bold adoration, the happiest two people Gus had ever seen.

"*Guster's Last Stand.* That is good," Roland said from somewhere in the room. "I like that."

Gus opened one eye and focused on the darkness around him. He could make out the rack of tire rims glinting from the bar lights. In the shadows he could see the outline of the motorcycle frames, the skeletons of old bikes filling the room, closing in on him. He thought about Sully's last words, how sad they were to listen to, and the promises he'd agreed to keep.

"Hey Roland, you can't sell them jackets," Gus was feeling sleepy, welcoming the rest. "And don't ask me to keep no secrets," he said and started dreaming.

In the dream Gus still had his ponytail. He was sitting at an outdoor cafe table with Sully, and the woman Gus had once been married to. A boy child was sitting in Sully's lap. The sun was warm, and everyone was happy. Gus liked the dream. Sully seemed to like it too, because he smiled, and squinted at the sun. Gus couldn't make out everything that Sully said as he stood up, holding out the boy towards Gus, but he thought he said *Go on, find your daddy.*

Every Person in the World

Comer sat at the bar watching the bartender crushing ice with a pestle and mortar.

"Are you in town for the races this weekend?" the bartender asked.

"No, I'm leaving in the morning," he answered, waiting for his bourbon.

"Have you been to the beach recently?" the bartender said.

"How's that?"

"You look like you've been in the sun."

"No, I've not been to the beach in a while," Comer wasn't much for making small talk, especially when he was working a job. The bartender considered him with a curious expression, trying to figure something out about him.

"Man, it must be nice having a complexion like yours, always with sun on your face even in November. You're lucky, you know that?" The bartender placed the heavy cut-glass tumbler on the varnished bar in front of him.

"I guess it depends on what you consider lucky," Comer said, lifting his glass. He left a twenty on the bar, took his leather portfolio of photographs, and walked towards the tables at the back of the room, the sharp report of his expensive shoes resounding much like the well shod horses he'd watched parading around the track.

Pausing at a line of photographs hanging on the wall, race day portraits of diminutive jockeys and their mounts, Comer thought how appropriate a place for the lovers' rendezvous. He drank his bourbon and appreciated again the feel of alcohol. He'd given it up because he knew it was the one thing that might get the best of him. He was sure his face was as red as a pomegranate, the effect of the bourbon making his cheeks blossom with the rush of blood. Comer noticed his reflected image in the glass of the framed picture and he brushed his whitening hair away from his forehead and looked around the room for a comfortable vantage point.

People from all over the world were in Louisville to watch the week of races leading up to the Breeder's Cup. He'd never spent much time at the track, or around horse people, but it was his reason for being there: to document the activities of a married woman who photographed horses, and a married man who made saddles and bridles, and both of them married to someone else. It was tawdry business, but it meant high-end accommodations. During his three days on this job, he had broken a twenty-year abstinence, taking up drinking again, and he liked it.

Two men in suits took seats at the end of the bar. Their voices and cheap shoes told him they were from the Eastern Bloc, possibly Russians. The small room resonated with the timbre of foreign accents. Comer liked the anonymity of his work. He found satisfaction in being inconspicuous, especially around privileged people. He'd made many problems go away for his employer, and the situations he'd been entrusted to resolve always gave him a feeling of purpose. At one time he envied the men who were the focus of his surveillances, but those feelings were now tempered with disdain after so many years of witnessing what a mess people could make of their lives.

As he walked around the room examining photographs, his

footsteps fell heavily on the pegged planks. He kept his shoes in immaculate condition. Stacked heels and leather sole cordovan slip-ons gave sturdy balance to his work attire. He wore tailored grey flannel trousers, a starched button down with a maroon and gold tie, and a cobalt toned cashmere blazer, all to be left behind when the job came to an end.

The overhead panels, draped in silk jerseys and horse banners, made appropriately dim lighting for the task at hand. He was there to wait for his employer's daughter-in-law to arrive with her lover, a man she'd spent three days with at the track and slept with in this hotel.

Comer chose a place in the back corner and took a seat where he could survey the room. He placed the portfolio of photographs on the table and took a deep drink of the bourbon. He didn't know if it was the alcohol, or the fact that he despised his employer's son, but he was losing interest in this assignment. He was ready to have it over with and spend a few days in a warm place sitting in the sun, allowing the tan to deepen the rouge of his winter face, to conceal the burst capillaries from years of hypertension. The bartender's misplaced compliment was one Comer had heard before, but now it was less amusing. In his line of work curious attention from strangers wasn't to his advantage.

A group of Saudi men loudly entered the bar. He watched them flounce across the room, wearing expensive thin-soled Italian loafers, their head covers and robes billowing. He wondered if their wealth brought them any more contentment than he'd noticed in the man he worked for. The Saudis had barely taken their seats before two bartenders arrived, with trays of pear-shaped glasses and two bottles. They arranged the snifters in the middle of the table; the Saudis appeared comfortable with the prompt attention. He wondered if they owned this staid, old hotel.

In Comer's thirty-five years working for the mill he had made things more comfortable for his old friend, and he'd been compensated so well he could now quit if he wished. He knew he couldn't stay on, working for his employer's son. The boy's troubles began when he was sent away to boarding school. Since then, Comer's job had become a matter of getting the boy out of trouble, rescuing him from near catastrophe. Comer's career had come down to this: following the wife of his employer's son. The task was joyless, base, and common: the Devil's work.

Before Louisville, Comer thoroughly investigated the background of the wife's lover. He admired the skill demonstrated in the quality of the saddles and harnesses the young man created. He'd taken a humble family business, making working tack, and had built it into a lucrative enterprise providing superb equestrian leather and silver work to those who could afford the best. The man had a wife and three young children. He'd learned his father's business and helped it to prosper. Comer was certain his employer's son didn't possess the same qualities. Comer raised two fingers towards the bartender, gesturing at his near empty tumbler.

He'd loved his job when he first started. He'd had significant challenges: investigating claims of bid-rigging at auctions of textile machinery, stopping a hostile take-over by a group of Northern investors, facing-down executives from competing firms. Comer was a loyal employee, and he'd always honored the trust invested in him.

His initial job had been to defeat labor organizers who came to

Mill Creek in '73. They stirred up so much trouble that gunshots were fired in the mill parking lot between second and third shifts one evening. Comer had made that problem go away with no bloodshed, and no union vote. He knew he'd saved people's jobs and kept his boss happy. Local folks soon forgot about the Labor people's promises. And a twelve-year-old girl had accused one of the Yankees of inappropriate touching as she walked past their picket line on her way home from dance class.

Comer traveled much of his career, and in fine fashion. His preparation for each job included locating the best men's store in whatever city he'd been sent to and purchasing clothes he would wear for the assignment. At the end of the job he'd hang the garments in his hotel room closet with a pinned note asking that they be donated to charity. The only accessories he kept were English-made shoes and an alligator belt. The blanket company paid him back as a business expense. He never wore work clothes on his own time, and so kept his two worlds separate.

A different bartender came to his table.

"What can I get for you?" she asked.

"First off, what are the Saudis drinking?"

"It's one-hundred-year old Cognac, or some kind of liqueur. They flew it in on a private jet, two cases for the week. It is ridiculously expensive," the young woman said.

"How much are we talking about?"

"I was told $10,000 a bottle."

He looked at the group of men with their mustaches, some of them too black to be un-dyed.

"You got to be kidding me. Best bourbon in the world and those fags are drinking that shit. Unbelievable." He felt the booze. The girl stood looking at him for a moment.

"What can I bring you?" she asked

"Blanton's on crushed ice," he said.

"Would you like to charge this to your room?"

"No, I pay as I drink," he answered.

The girl turned towards the bar and Comer watched her stop at the Saudis' table to speak with them.

He never used credit cards. All of his transactions were conducted in cash, and the receipts turned over to the accounting people at the mill. Handling money repulsed him, but his mode of operation required a thick wad of currency which he kept folded in the breast pocket of his blazer. He reached inside his jacket, extracted two crisply folded one hundred dollar bills, and placed them on the table.

He waited for the couple to show up so he could seal the deal. He opened the folder of glossy prints intended to prove the couple's intimacy. He didn't have the *money shot* to prove a physical relationship, a failure that bothered him. Even so, he knew what they were up to, and he had enough evidence to nail them, to protect his employer's investments, and to save the son a great deal of soon-to-be-inherited money.

The first series of photographs were of the lover's leather works. Comer had gone to the area outside of the racetrack where vendors displayed their wares. The man brought his goods to Louisville in an expensive trailer with display racks of silver work, leather saddles, and harnesses. Comer asked permission to take pictures of the items to show a perspective client, and the young man had graciously agreed. He snapped a picture of the man adjusting a display of leather lead harnesses. He noticed that the man's well-worn boots were of fine quality. Shoes told a lot about a man in Comer's way of seeing the world. The fellow was sincere and handsome, accomplished in a way that extended beyond what he'd inherited. Comer enjoyed the smell of the leather.

"You ever get used to the smell?" he asked the younger man

"No," he'd said, "I love it, I never get used to it, but my wife can't smell it anymore."

"Is she with you on this trip?" Comer asked.

"No, she keeps the shop going when I'm out of town"

"That's too bad," Comer said.

He looked around for a few minutes longer, asked for a business card. The young man handed him the card and a catalogue containing slick, sharp photographs taken by the woman he was there to follow. Later, in his hotel room, Comer had studied the catalogue. Near the back of the book was a photograph of the man and his family, posed in front of his workshop. His wife and three children stood smiling in the sunshine, their handmade boots and belts gleaming. He kept the catalogue in the portfolio along with the other proof of the relationship he was there to expose. Comer noticed that the man's wife was attractive, not much different in appearance than the woman he was there to follow.

He looked at the next series of images. They were of the woman; her raven hair glistening in the morning sun as she stood on the damp dirt concourse leading to the track; of her talking with a small Hispanic man wearing a baseball cap; of her taking pictures of jockeys and horse people; of her wandering around the paddock area lugging photography gear; and of her and her lover in the back of a stall facing one another. He paused, lingering over this last photo.

The woman's lover held a lead rein in one hand, a plastic stadium cup in the other. Light shone down on the couple, illuminating their faces in a glow that defied the placement of the two standing in the back of the shadowy stall, distanced from the sun-lit day, something he had not noticed when he framed them in the lens. He studied the man's cheeks, creased from time in the sun, and the glint of his teeth as he smiled at the woman. In the photograph she tilted her head slightly, her chin pointing at her lover's face looking at him sideways, her long and delicate fingers touching the tip of the leather harness he held in his hand, her eyes and mouth defying any effort to hide a deep admiration, a shared interest in whatever it was they were discussing. Two people as fit and attractive as adult humans could possibly be. He removed the picture from the others and set it aside.

He returned the two paper-clipped stacks of images to the portfolio and took up the last series of photographs. These were taken in the hotel room the woman reserved in her name. He was surprised at how easily he'd gained access to the room.

On the second morning, once he knew the couple was at the track, he walked the two blocks from the Browne Hotel to the Seelbach. He climbed the carpeted stairway instead of taking the old brass elevator. No one took notice of him. He was just a well-dressed, red faced older gentleman, his white hair hand-brushed from his forehead; no one suspected his intentions. The room service women pushed stacked carts of fresh linens down the hallway, quietly knocking on doors, making sure guests had vacated before entering. Comer approached a woman, who looked like a latino.

"*Con permiso,*" he said "*Mi llave esta en mi habitacion. Puedes abrir mi puerta con la llave, por favor?*" He needed, he said, to get into his room and he'd left his room key in another jacket. Could she let him in? He made the motion of turning a key in a lock.

The woman smiled at Comer. He felt he might earn her trust by speaking to her in Spanish, but she shook her head.

"*Lo siento, señor. No tengo permiso para hacerlo. Usted debe ir a la recepción.*" She couldn't, she was sorry to say, open the door for anyone. But he could get another key at the reception desk. She pointed toward the hotel lobby as she spoke.

Comer smiled back, put one hand to his forehead in a gesture of forgetfulness, and reached into his pocket with the other hand to fetch a twenty dollar bill.

"*Soy muy olvidadizo ultimamente. La distancia a la recepcion es mucho y yo soy un Viejo.*" "But it is such a long way for an old man to walk," he said, and held the smooth bill in his hand, extending it towards her. "*Por favor.*"

She took the money, and asked him which room he was staying in. Comer led her the short distance down the hall, and watched as she took the loop of keys from the lanyard around her neck and unlocked the latch.

"*Muchas gracias,*" he said, as he turned to enter the room where his employer's daughter-in-law had committed adultery.

He photographed the unmade bed, the faint imprint of two bodies upon the rumpled sheets, the gift wrapping paper left on the floor, the empty bottle of champagne, the two flutes on the bedside table. In the bathroom he photographed evidence of a man in the room, and the contents of the refuse can under the bathroom vanity. He photographed a hand-written card that went with the wrapping paper, the lines of perfect feminine script--- *You make this world right.*

The barkeep brought a fresh drink. "Anything else I can get for you?" she asked.

"Yes, take a round, the same as I'm drinking, to the gentlemen at the table over there." He pointed towards the Saudis, handed the girl the two bills.

"Anything else?" she asked.

"Not right now, but thanks for your help." He took a sip from his drink while the girl returned to the bar, the Saudis laughed loudly, and the room suddenly shrunk around him.

He thought about his walk back to his hotel a couple of blocks away. It was the other grand old place in town, and along the way he would pass a historic marker he noticed on his first day in Louisville. It told of a man having an epiphany at that spot. The man realized he loved every person in the world, and then had removed himself to a monastery and become a writer and theologian. Comer wasn't familiar with the story, and as he looked around he wondered how a mundane intersection might have inspired such a conversion. The sign referred to the "Louisville Epiphany," and it made him consider a person's capacity for change.

The bartender approached the Saudis with a silver serving tray; on it were the drinks Comer had ordered for them. He observed their dismayed reactions. The server nodded in his direction, and the Saudis looked his way. He smiled, gave an effete wave of his hand. The bartender left the tray of drinks on the table and came towards Comer.

"The gentlemen send their most respectful thanks," she said, then returned to her business behind the bar.

He was becoming distracted by the activities in the bar, and too comfortable from the bourbon. He leaned back in his chair and pushed the packet of photographs across the table, as far away from him as he could. He picked up the one photograph he'd set aside, and studied it again. Something about it unsettled him. The glow of the couple's faces, the length of their bodies, their shared admiration, made him feel something he'd never felt for any of the other people he'd been sent to follow. He was reluctant to include the picture in the report he would turn over to his employer, because he'd missed something in his observations, and he wasn't able to figure out what it was. He looked up from the picture just as the couple entered the room.

He noticed how they stopped to survey their surroundings, she just slightly ahead of her lover, his fingertips lightly brushing her elbow as he whispered into her ear, the way she smiled at him and nodded towards a booth not far from the bar. He observed the calm grace, the physicality of their motion. He leaned back in his chair, placed his palms on the table, and exhaled in response to the glow he saw again, the radiance he'd seen first in the photograph, and now again. Anyone would have noticed the arc of energy, the mutual respect and the affection captured in the photograph sitting on his table. As they made their way across the room, he couldn't help but smile and shake his head. They slid into the booth across from one another. What a beautiful pair they made, as honestly given over to their attraction as people could be.

He watched the couple place their order, and considered how a woman like her could have married a man like his employer's son, a simple, disinterested boy who didn't share his wife's interests. He knew other attractive women who'd married ordinary and dull men. He'd dealt with it before in his job, but this was the first time he'd been sent to discredit a wife. Many times he'd been dispatched to find out what mill executives did when they were out of town, or to investigate the character of men who were being considered for positions with the company. He was familiar with that, and comfortable exposing indiscretions, but this was a much different situation.

He wondered if the woman knew about her husband's golf weekends away with his buddies, or the escort service girls he had flown in from Atlanta, or about the former babysitter whose tuition was being taken care of after her husband made more of a drunken late night drive home than he should have, or the lake house kept for another girl, or about her husband's cavalier attitude towards money and responsibility and his selfish reasons for asking his father to send Comer on this trip. He could tell her all of this, but it wasn't what he was being paid to do.

"Is there anything else I can do for you?" the bartender asked.

"Could you please bring me a plastic cup?" he asked.

"My pleasure." The girl looked at him with a slack expression, and he thought she didn't seem an appropriate employee for this kind of place.

He handed her another twenty-dollar bill and waved her away.

The couple settled into their booth. Comer appreciated their daring, to have fallen in love despite all of the risks. For a brief moment he envied the man's youth, his ability to make things of great value, and he admired the woman for her determination to pursue the passion she didn't share with her husband.

He thought about the concept of love. Why love everyone in the world? Wouldn't it be enough to feel in love with just one person? The answer was beyond his knowing.

The roar of the Saudis did not seem to distract the woman as she talked to her lover. Comer watched her using her hands to gesture as she spoke, long fingers mimicking the click of the camera button, her lover leaning forward, then back and using his hands to approximate the cinching of a bridle. They were talking about work, their shared passion. His waitress returned with the cup.

He poured from the crystal glass into the plastic cup and looked at the photograph of the lovers smiling at one another. Across the bottom of the photograph he wrote with a felt tipped pen, *What a pair!* He took the catalogue from the portfolio, slid the photograph into the front pages of the book.

The Saudi men were laughing, consumed with their own significance. Comer took his drink and began walking across the room. He stopped at their table and noticed their dainty liqueurs, the expensive bourbon he'd sent to their table sitting untouched on the serving tray. The men looked at Comer with impassive black eyes. He'd interrupted their good time.

"You boys are drinking horse piss," he said.

The men stared at Comer, and he felt impelled to offend them further.

"You're in Louisville, Kentucky, goddamn it. Not Monte Carlo, for Christ's sake."

He slapped the closest Saudi on the back and didn't smile "Drink up!" he said.

He turned away from the silent table and made his way towards the couple. He focused on their faces.

"Pardon me," Comer said. He spoke to the man and held out the catalogue "I came by your display the other day and I had a couple of questions I wanted to ask you. May I?" Comer looked to the woman, her face still smiling, and then back to the man.

"Sure, have a seat."

An awkward moment of silence followed as Comer joined them in the booth. He extended the moment by placing the catalogue on the table, and set his plastic cup towards the edge. No introductions were made, but Comer looked to the woman and pursed his lips in a sad smile.

"What can I do for you?" the younger man asked.

"This is sure a nice catalogue you've put together," Comer said. "Who took all the photographs?"

"She did," the man said, and nodded to the woman across the table.

When Comer looked at her this time her expression was blank. She was studying him.

"You are a fine photographer," he said to the woman. She did not respond. Her eyes were intently watching Comer as if she knew he was not stopping to chat about saddles.

He opened the catalogue and flipped through a few pages "This is all really fine stuff you make, just terrific. You have a nice shop and you must be doing very well." Comer kept turning the pages until he came to the photograph of the man and his family. "Is this your wife and kids?"

"Mike, don't say anything else to this man," the woman spoke for the first time.

"Pardon me?" Comer said.

"Look, I know who you are. I don't know your name, but I know who you work for, and what you do for a living." Her eyes welled with tears, but her voice was steady, and Comer noticed that her throat had become blotched. She folded her long arms across her chest and sat back in the booth, tilted her head, and disdainfully considered Comer.

"I'm not sure I understand what's going on here," the younger man said.

Comer watched as she bit her trembling lip. "Hey, let's don't be sad," Comer said. "I've got something I want to give you." He took the photograph from the catalogue and placed it in front of the woman. She looked down at the image of her and her lover, and a tear traced her cheek. He watched her look at her lover as she turned the photograph around for him to inspect. She glanced at Comer and he felt her contempt.

"You can leave now," she said.

Comer turned to the man sitting next to him. He looked prepared for whatever would happen.

"I can't imagine not being able to appreciate the smell of leather anymore," Comer said to the man.

"What is it you want from us?" the man asked.

Comer stood next to the booth and took his time studying both of their faces once again before placing the leather portfolio under his arm and taking the plastic cup of chipped ice and bourbon in his hand. "I don't want anything from you or anyone else." Comer smiled, but he was no longer proud that he could make problems go away

He walked through the lobby and down the curved marble steps passing the large portraits of long dead Louisville society people, and he timed the spin of the revolving door so as to not break his stride on his way out to the street that ended on the banks of the Ohio River.

Comer felt the bourbon bloom of his face and was relieved to have finished the job inside of the Seelbach Hotel bar. The crisp night air invigorated him, and he headed away from the river towards his hotel room. After a couple of blocks he approached the intersection where the other man's epiphany had taken place. He stopped again to read the words on the sign. He doubted anyone's ability to truly love everyone in the world; it seemed a grandiose proclamation. Possibly two people could honestly love one another, maybe that was more of an epiphany than to renounce worldly desires in the name of one's love for all humanity.

He glanced up and down the vacant street, no horse carriages or people were out at this time of night. A half a block away from the sign he noticed a steel girded trash bin. He took the photographs he'd taken of the hotel room and the three page report of the lovers' weekend, and dropped them into the refuse pile. He could provide his employer evidence that the two people were doing their work and that their jobs brought them together, and then remove himself from their lives.

He walked along to the cadence of his soles clapping on the cold November concrete. He considered what type of shoes a monk would wear in a monastery. He imagined sandals, or some other type of footwear representing a surrender of worldly desires. The night gave Comer a feeling close to contentment. He decided to walk for a while longer, with no destination in mind, just the satisfaction of knowing that he had no reason for envy, of anyone.

Acknowledgments

I owe gratitude to the writers who encouraged me to stick to the solitary task of writing fiction; Gail Galloway Adams, Rand Richards Cooper, Keith Flynn, Eugene B. Hoch, Ron Rash, Michel Smoak Stone, Luke Whisnant, Steve Yarbrough.

A special thanks to Tim Peeler for bolstering me during my darkest days.

To Cindy, Carter and Jack, thank you for providing what I've most needed---the comfort of family.

About the Author

David Dickson entered the world in 1963 at Perrin Field in Grayson County, Texas. Born to a Fighter Pilot father, his mother was a musical Savant. He has one sibling, an older sister. The product of the North Carolina Public Education System, David spent 27 years as a High School History teacher. He divides his time between Texas and North Carolina as the father of two sons. The stories in this collection were written in North Carolina.

Made in the USA
Middletown, DE
20 May 2024

54317173R00092